Michael Underwood and The Murder Room

>>> This title is part of The Murder Room, our series dedicated to making available out-of-print or hard-to-find titles by classic crime writers.

Crime fiction has always held up a mirror to society. The Victorians were fascinated by sensational murder and the emerging science of detection; now we are obsessed with the forensic detail of violent death. And no other genre has so captivated and enthralled readers.

Vast troves of classic crime writing have for a long time been unavailable to all but the most dedicated frequenters of second-hand bookshops. The advent of digital publishing means that we are now able to bring you the backlists of a huge range of titles by classic and contemporary crime writers, some of which have been out of print for decades.

From the genteel amateur private eyes of the Golden Age and the femmes fatales of pulp fiction, to the morally ambiguous hard-boiled detectives of mid twentieth-century America and their descendants who walk our twenty-first century streets, The Murder Room has it all. >>>

The Murder Room
Where Criminal Minds Meet

themurderroom.com

Michael Underwood (1916–1992)

Michael Underwood (the pseudonym of John Michael Evelyn) was born in Worthing, Sussex and educated at Christ Church College, Oxford. He was called to the Bar in 1939 and served in the British army during World War Two. He returned to work in the Department of Public Prosecutions until his retirement in 1976, and wrote almost 50 crime novels informed by his career in the law. His five series characters include Sergeant Nick Atwell and lawyer Rosa Epton, of whom is was said by the *Washington Post* that she 'outdoes Perry Mason'.

By Michael Underwood

Lawful Pursuit

Michael Underwood

An Orion book

Copyright © Isobel Mackenzie 1958

The right of Michael Underwood to be identified as the author of this
work has been asserted in accordance with the Copyright, Designs and
Patents Act 1988.

This edition published by
The Orion Publishing Group Ltd
Orion House
5 Upper St Martin's Lane
London WC2H 9EA

An Hachette UK company
A CIP catalogue record for this book is available from the British Library

ISBN 978 1 4719 0772 2

www.orionbooks.co.uk

To Dorothy Gardiner

CHAPTER ONE

The bit of wall against which Detective Superintendent Manton now surreptitiously leaned was the court-room's most favoured observation post, and three sets of marks on the oak pannelling testified to this. Head high, the wood had, over the years, become darkened from constant massage with cheap hair oil: midway between this patch and the floor was a lighter area where well-cushioned behinds had had the opposite effect: and at heel height was an ugly pattern of black streaks and scratches.

Manton shifted his weight imperceptibly so as not to give the impression of slouching; a thing he disapproved of in court, especially by police officers. Moreover, Lord Droxford, the presiding magistrate at West End Magistrates' Court, though a humane and kindly man, was a stickler for the proprieties when he was on the bench.

At the present moment there was a lull in proceedings and the dock was unoccupied. Lord Droxford was bent over the large court register on the desk before him. Mr. Astbury, the chief clerk, was vainly trying to attract the attention of Arnold Plowman, the court usher, who was engrossed in a seemingly endless mimed interchange with someone in the public standing room at the back.

Manton surveyed the scene and waited. He knew quite well what was going to happen and this made him wonder whether his journey had been really necessary, albeit one involving only a fourpenny bus fare. Any minute now, the swing door beside him, which led to the jailer's office and the cells beyond, would fly-open and the large blue figure of P.C. Tredgold would thrust through.

In the meantime, silence reigned in court, broken only by the melancholy notes outside, of old Susannah's accordion. Being like most of the English race, inflexibly sentimental at heart, Manton, as he listened, experienced a surge of simple pride that a busy London court allowed an old Negress street musician to have her pitch immediately outside its doors. But the truth was that West End was a happy court and that Susannah had almost come to be regarded as one of its permanent staff.

1

Lord Droxford looked up from his register, a slightly impatient gleam in his eye. He was forestalled from translating this into words, however, by the bustling entrance of P.C. Tredgold.

'Number three remand, sir, Alexander Constantine Brufa. No appearance.'

Thus delivered, the jailer threw Manton a quick, meaning look and waited to see how the magistrate and his clerk proposed to play the ball he'd just bowled them. Lord Droxford studied the register once more.

'A charge of living on the immoral earnings, I see,' he said thoughtfully.

Mr. Astbury in his seat immediately below the bench half turned.

'You gave him bail, sir, in his own recognizance of two hundred and fifty pounds and there was a surety in the same amount.'

'Is the officer in charge of the case in court?' Lord Droxford asked and looked up to see Mr. Rex Turnbull hovering before him in the lawyer's pew. 'Are you in this case, Mr. Turnbull?'

'I really find myself in a most awkward situation, sir,' Mr. Turnbull began, looking a picture of unhappiness. Lord Droxford smiled at him amiably and reflected how rich he could have been if he'd collected half a crown every time Mr. Turnbull had used the expression as a preface to explaining the behaviour of one of his clients. 'I was instructed by Mr. Brufa after his last appearance before you, sir, when you remanded him till today so that he could be legally represented. I'm at a complete loss to know why he isn't here, and I can only suppose he must have got confused over the dates. . . . Unless he's somewhere outside all the time and hasn't heard his name called.'

Mr. Turnbull looked hopefully towards the door which led into the main hall and Lord Droxford nodded at Plowman, the usher, who was waiting for the cue and left the court. A moment later, resounding cries of 'Alexander Constantine Brufa' filled the building. Plowman reappeared.

'No answer, sir,' he reported in the satisfied tone of someone who has successfully accomplished a difficult assignment.

'He hasn't been seen at any of his usual haunts during the past week, sir.' This blunt assertion of fact came from Detective Sergeant Cloud, who had come round to the witness box to make certain he too had his say. He was the officer in charge of the case and felt considerably aggrieved since he had opposed

2

bail in the first place; so that none of this would have happened if the court had paid greater heed to his views.

'Haunts being his home and place of employment, I take it?' Lord Droxford said.

'His lodgings, and the cafés and clubs he frequents, sir.' Then in a tone charged with significance, Sergeant Cloud added: 'He didn't have any regular employment.'

'No, er—I see; presumably not,' Lord Droxford replied, recalling the nature of the charge. 'Have you any reason to believe he's left the country, Sergeant? What about his passport? Didn't I order that to be surrendered as one of the conditions of bail?'

'Yes, sir, and I have it here.'

'M'mm. Well, there's nothing I can do except issue a warrant for his arrest, I suppose.'

'The surety?' Mr. Astbury hissed over his shoulder.

'Oh, yes! Is the surety here?'

Sergeant Cloud beckoned to a small, sallow, worried-looking man who was standing near the dock.

'Are you the person who went bail for Alexander Brufa?' asked Mr. Astbury.

The man rolled his eyes and nodded.

'Any reason why you shouldn't forfeit two hundred and fifty pounds?' Lord Droxford chimed in. 'You undertook to see that Brufa attended court today and we've just been told that he's disappeared.'

'I donnta know whaire 'e go,' the man said with an effort.

'I dare say you don't, but it looks as though his absence is going to cost you two hundred and fifty pounds. I'll have to think about that, and I'll give my decision later. Meanwhile, let's get on with the next case.'

There was a general stir in which the hapless surety was hustled away by Sergeant Cloud.

Manton remained leaning quietly against the wall. As expected, he'd learnt nothing he hadn't already known.

It might seem that there was nothing very remarkable in what had happened: in an accused man jumping bail.

There wasn't—except that Brufa was the sixth to vanish in such circumstances in as many months. And all from the same court, too.

3

CHAPTER TWO

Manton was about to slip out of court when P.C. Tredgold reappeared with the next defendant. It was Joe Mendolia, who was as well known at West End Court as Susannah.

Without waiting to be bidden Mendolia stepped fastidiously into the small railed dock, giving Manton no more than a cursory glance as his gaze roamed over the faces of those around him. Though the two of them had never met, each had made it his business to know something of the other.

Manton, for example, in common with anyone who could read a newspaper, knew that Mendolia was one of the so-called Kings of Soho who made a good thing out of other people's vices. So good that he was able to live in a luxury flat, drive around in a cyclamen-pink sports car (but one of three cars he owned), buy diamonds for his lady-friends and all the while remain beyond the law's main reach.

Manton studied him covertly as he stood in the dock, elegantly resting his well-manicured hands on the rail in front of him. He was wearing a deep blue light-weight suit with white silk shirt and a silver-and-pink tie. He gave the impression of having just stepped out of Cellophane wrapping and brought with him the delicate aroma of attar of roses.

The reason for his presence in the dock, Manton now learnt, was one of the more flagrant breaches of the licensing laws at one of the prosperous, subterranean clubs he owned in the district.

When the charge had been read out, Mr. Turnbull rose to his feet.

'I appear in this case, sir, and there's a plea of guilty.'

After Lord Droxford had been briefly appraised of the facts by the prosecuting solicitor, Mr Turnbull rose again.

'This is a most unfortunate affair, sir, but one which I hope you will feel you can properly regard as a mere technical breach of the law by my client. Let me at once say, sir, that Mr. Mendolia was greatly distressed when he learnt what had happened and that he took prompt steps to ensure that nothing of the sort could occur again. . . .'

Since everyone in court, including Mr. Turnbull to whose profit it was, knew that Joe Mendolia was as indifferent to the laws of the land as a pagan to Easter Mass, there was something of an air of unreality about this plea. While it was going on, Mendolia, however, stood preening himself like a bird, waiting patiently for it to finish. He patted his hip pocket to make sure that the roll of fivers he'd brought to pay the fine with was still there. Then he turned to survey the public behind him and winked lazily on spotting one of his henchmen.

As Manton watched him, an idea started forming at the back of his mind. It was interrupted, however, by Lord Droxford suddenly saying:

'There'll be a fine of one hundred pounds and you must also pay twenty-five guineas costs.' He looked towards Mr. Turnbull and added in a dry tone: 'I take it your client doesn't ask for time to pay?'

But before the solicitor had time to turn and consult him, Mendolia was half-way out of court, brazenly counting five-pound notes as he went.

Manton followed him into the jailer's office, where there was the usual throng of police officers and defendants. A respectful hush attended Mendolia's arrival at the counter where a sergeant was on duty collecting fines.

'Here's your lolly for you,' Mendolia said cheerfully, as he threw down twenty-six brand-new five-pound notes. He watched with a tolerant smile as the officer held each up to the light and carefully examined the watermark. Then he turned to Manton. 'Suspicious lot of b——s in this place, aren't they? Wish I *could* make 'em as good as that. It'd help solve a lot of life's little problems.'

'Mean to say forgery's something you *haven't* yet had a go at?' the sergeant asked casually as he continued his examination of the notes.

'I imagine he makes enough without the need,' Manton observed.

'Hey, whose side are you on? And anyway, what's brought Scotland Yard out slumming today?'

Manton recognized the note of interest in the second question. He shrugged his shoulders.

'Merely taking a look around.'

'Yeah? Just the weather for it, too, isn't it?' Mendolia laughed loudly at his own remark.

'Here's your change. Three pounds fifteen shillings,' the sergeant said, pushing the money across the counter. Mendolia

5

pocketed the coins, but looked with distaste at the crumpled bank-notes.

'At least nobody could accuse you of running *this* lot off on your little home press. Where the hell do you get such stinking bits of paper?' He held up one of the pound notes of his change with an air of mock despair. It had been torn diagonally down the centre and the two halves ineptly rejoined. 'Just take a look at this one; almost seems like the two halves don't want to know each other?' He tossed it back. 'Here, you keep it.'

'Keep it?'

'Yeah, give it to your orphans and widows fund.'

'You give it to your own something orphans,' the sergeant growled angrily. 'We don't need your charity to keep us alive.'

Mendolia treated his audience to a resigned shrug and stuffed the note in on top of the rest of the change in his trouser pocket. Next, he thoughtfully studied the wafer-thin gold watch on his left wrist.

'A quarter to one. I guess it's time to leave you boys to your buns and cocoa.'

With an airy gesture of the hand he made his farewell and departed, leaving the sergeant muttering darkly under his breath and Manton staring after him in a preoccupied way.

Outside, old Susannah was singing one of her specials, whose tune had a fieriness well suited to the revivalist theme of its words. She presented a curious picture perched on her camp-stool with her feet neatly resting together on the little wooden platform which she always used to keep them off the ground.

A Negro with white hair is a striking figure, and a Negress even more so. Thus was Susannah, adorned further by a battered mauve hat and the thickest pair of spectacles anyone had ever seen. Why she wore them, nobody knew, as they availed her nothing; for several years she had been totally blind.

Joe Mendolia was about to pass her by, when he suddenly stopped, dived a hand into his pocket and brought out the torn piece of money.

'Here you are, old girl, have this. No one else seems to want it.' He stuffed it into the tin mug which hung loosely from the accordion.

Like a spider which has felt a pull at its web, one black hand shot out, retrieved the note, swiftly valued it and tucked it deep away among the voluminous garments.

CHAPTER THREE

On leaving court, Manton went straight back to the Yard and, after a quick meal in the canteen, up to his room to await a summons from the Assistant Commissioner (Crime). This came about the middle of the afternoon, and he immediately went along to the great man's room, which lay on the Embankment side of the building and had a fine sweeping view of the river, including Westminster Bridge and, over on the south side, the handsome façade of County Hall.

'Sit down and make yourself comfortable. I must just sign these letters,' the A.C. said after Manton had entered. A minute later, he pushed them on one side and looked up. 'Now let's hear the latest. But first of all, are we agreed that these disappearances are not a series of isolated coincidences?'

'I'm positive they're connected, sir.'

'You've checked on backgrounds, of course?'

'Yes, sir, thoroughly. Admittedly all six defendants did live or work in Soho, but there isn't a scrap of evidence that they frequented the same places, still less that they knew each other. The only common factor in their lives, sir, is West End Court.'

'H'mm! Plus their foreign-sounding names, don't forget, and the fact they've all since ended up in Algeria.'

Manton glanced down at the file on his lap. 'Vapilos, Apel, Plaxides, Averoff, Osuna and Brufa,' he read out.

'Certainly couldn't find six less Anglo-Saxon than that,' the A.C. murmured, pursing his lips in a thoughtful way. 'The last two sound like a vaudeville act. Well! What do you suggest?' he asked, looking up suddenly.

For the next ten minutes, Manton outlined his plan. When he finished speaking, there was a short silence. Then the A.C. said:

'We've obviously got to do something about it, and I think your plan is likely to bring quick results. If it doesn't come off, that'll be that, and we'll have to tackle the problem another way. But we can't let this sort of thing go on.'

He picked up the telephone and spoke to a number of his departmental chiefs issuing the necessary orders. The result was that soon after Manton got back to his own room there was a knock on the door and Detective Constables Cordari and Swift came in.

7

Both were on the short side, dark and in their mid-twenties; but there the similarity ended. Roy Cordari was slight in build and had a sallow, Mediterranean appearance, being indeed only one generation removed from that part of the world. He spoke fluent Italian and modern Greek and was a member of the Special Branch. Kevin Swift was more compact, had a fresh, clean look about him and sported a hair style just the right side of a crew cut. He was one of the young detective officers of the central pool at Scotland Yard known as C.I.

Neither knew the other except by sight and neither had the faintest notion why he had now been sent for. As soon as they were seated, Manton opened the proceedings.

'I don't know whether either of you has heard about some disappearances over the past few months from West End Court of defendants on bail? There've been six altogether and it now seems pretty certain that at any rate five of them have been smuggled out of the country.' He drew his legs under his chair and leant forward to add emphasis to his words. 'The sixth man failed to answer to his bail only this morning. We heard a day or so ago that he hadn't been seen around, and so we weren't very surprised when he didn't turn up at court today. The point is, the A.C. has now decided that it's time to launch a full-scale inquiry into what's going on.' He paused and looked from one to the other of the two alert faces before him. 'I've been put in charge of the investigation and you've been assigned to work with me.' He was quick to notice their looks of surprise and added: 'In fact you've both been specially recommended to the A.C. for the job. Now I'd better tell you what the plan is. By the way, smoke if you want to.' Cordari shook his head and murmured something from which Manton gathered he didn't. Swift pulled out a pipe. Manton watched him lighting it for a moment and decided that if he was as competent at detection as he was at getting a pipe going, he must be quite a bright young man. 'The broad idea is this: that you, Cordari, should act as a decoy. We'll give you a new name and a new background and in due course you're going to appear at West End Court charged with a suitable offence. Beyond that it's impossible to see at present, but the hope is, of course, that if we make you a sort of composite of the six men who've already vanished, someone will try to interest you too in a trip abroad. There's still a mass of detail we'll have to work out together, but it'll probably mean your being installed in a room in Soho for a week or so beforehand, in order to provide you with the necessary local ties. It wouldn't do just to produce you out of nowhere and pop you in the dock.'

'Who's going to be on this at West End, sir?' Cordari asked quickly.

'No one. In fact, one of the reasons you two have been picked is because neither of you is known at that court. That is so by the way, isn't it?'

'Never set foot inside there, sir,' Swift said.

'Nor have I.' Then in a slightly anxious tone, Cordari added: 'But if the magistrate isn't even to know it's a put-up job, what guarantee is there that he'll allow me bail?'

Manton grinned. 'It'll be darned unlucky for you if he doesn't, won't it? But, seriously, I don't think you need worry about that. We'll be able to pitch the thing so that he does.'

'Are you going to be the officer in charge of the case that's put up against me, sir?'

'No, I shall be keeping well out of sight. It'll probably be Detective Sergeant Talper. He, of course, will be in the know, but otherwise no one, except us three and the big brass here.'

'Where exactly do I come into this, sir?' Swift asked.

'You'll be Cordari's shadow and also general contact man between him and us here at the Yard. I need hardly say that the whole success of the operation, if it ever gets going, will rest on your combined abilities to lull the enemy into a false sense of security.'

While Cordari appeared impassive, so that Manton found it difficult to judge his reaction to the scheme, Swift was obviously excited about its thrillerish aspects and the prospect of a break with normal Yard routine.

'Either of you married?' Manton asked, realizing that this might explain their different reactions.

'I am sir,' Cordari said.

'How long?'

'Two years.'

'Any children?'

'A baby girl. She'll be a year old on the eighth of next month.'

'No, sir,' Swift said, when Manton looked at him.

'Engaged?'

'Not even that, sir.' He grinned. 'But don't think I'm a woman-hater.'

'That's reassuring, anyway,' Manton remarked dryly. He

looked thoughtful and then turned slowly back to Cordari. 'I've really no right to say this, but are you quite happy about the role you're going to have to play? I mean——'

'Happy about it?' Cordari sounded genuinely surprised.

'Yes, It's going to be very much like walking a tight-rope in the dark and——'

Again Cordari cut him short. 'It was the element of excitement and not knowing from day to day what the next would bring that got me into the police. Don't worry about me, sir, nor about my being married. Doreen's already a well-trained policeman's wife.'

'Fine,' Manton said with a measure of relief. 'And now I'd better tell you what we do know about the matter.'

For the next twenty minutes or so he related all the known facts, while Cordari and Swift listened intently. When he had finished, he said:

'So the pattern which emerges is this. Each of these defendants was male and each stood charged with an offence involving one of the more profitable forms of vice, in respect of which he was liable to go inside for quite a spell. In addition each of them had a foreign-sounding name and either lived or traded in the Soho area. Hence their allegiance to West End Court.'

'Have there been similar disappearances from any of the other Magistrates' Courts during the same period, sir?' Swift broke in.

'No. West End's the only one.'

'Significant, sir, that, isn't it?'

'I agree. And even more so is that they've all be spirited away to the same place, too. Namely, Algeria. In every instance they've turned up there within a week or ten days of vanishing from here.'

'And after that, sir, nothing, I gather?' Cordari said.

'Complete silence. That is, so far as we know. As you can imagine, their relatives haven't been exactly forthcoming, but it has been ascertained that five of them—that is, everyone except the chap today, who's hardly had time to arrive anywhere —sent letters from Algeria telling their families not to worry and saying that chummy would be getting in touch again shortly.'

'There's no doubt about the letters being genuine, sir?' Cordari asked.

'None. The writing in every case has been identified as that of the fugitive concerned. No, these chaps have all got to Algeria all right. How and what then, is what I hope we're going to be able to discover.'

'What about the police out there, sir?' Swift said. 'Have they been asked to help at all?'

'Oh, yes, we've been in touch with them via Interpol. But these indirect, long-distance approaches are never very satis-factory, as you can probably guess. Especially in this case, seeing that the French authorities out there have enough on their plate with terrorists and the like without bothering overmuch about a handful of missing Britons. But we did tell them all we knew, which was precious little, and got a reply saying that there was no record of any such persons arriving in or leaving Algeria.'

'Do they keep records of every single arrival in the country, sir?' Swift asked.

'I gather so, but since our five obviously wouldn't have been travelling under their own names, it proves nothing. I should think it's also more than probable they were armed with other than British passports.' He shook his head. 'No, I doubt whether Interpol can help us much in this.'

Swift tapped his teeth with the stem of his pipe. 'And you believe, sir, that Mendolia may be behind a racket to smuggle wanted men out of the country?'

'All I can really say is that it's right up his street. There's no suggestion he's been mixed up in anything of the sort before, but it's obviously a well-organized and money-making racket.' Manton paused here, and then said determinedly: 'And that means a Mendolia type of racket. These six chaps who've dis-appeared all had money, and I don't doubt they've paid through the nose to be spirited away. False passports and the like are always costly items. Indeed, one thing that sticks out a mile is that apparently only those well spliced with cash have been approached.' He looked across at Cordari. 'We shall have to put you in the money class, too.'

'Make it enough, sir, and you'll have a seventh disappearance to investigate.'

Manton laughed. 'Incidentally, there is another feature of the case which I haven't yet mentioned. Only one of these six was not legally represented at court. The remainder were all clients of Mr. Rex Turnbull, who also happens to be *Mendolia's* solicitor.'

11

'Where are Turnbull's offices, sir?'

'Directly opposite West End Court.'

There ensued a thoughtful silence, which was broken by Cordari.

'What puzzles me most, sir, is why they should all have gone to Algeria. After all, it's got no connections with this country and, from what I've read in the papers recently, it's one helluva place to avoid.'

'Presumably the organization that's operating this racket has a convenient branch out there,' Manton said, and made a helpless gesture. 'It must be something like that, for I don't imagine that they just cast up their clients on any old sandy shore and leave them to get on with it.'

'It may be just a staging post, sir; a kind of transit camp where fugitives from justice are sorted and readdressed.'

'God knows what it is; or what they do when they get there—beyond posting a letter home.'

Cordari looked out of the window with an almost dreamy expression.

'The weather should be perfect by the time *I* arrive. And there's nothing to beat a Mediterranean spring.'

'Isn't part of the Sahara in Algeria?' Swift asked in a tone of sweet innocence. Manton appeared not to hear this remark, his mind being busy elsewhere, and Cordari contented himself with mouthing a short but pungent comment.

CHAPTER FOUR

Much of the next two days was spent in Manton's office, working out details of the plan.

It was decided that Cordari should be metamorphosed into Rafaele Skourasi, of Italian–Lebanese parentage, and that he should rent a room above a Turkish Cypriot tailor's shop just off Wardour Street. Furthermore, that in about ten days' time he should be brought up at West End Court on a charge of drug peddling. Not too serious a one (otherwise Lord Droxford might refuse him bail), but with a quiet hint, to anyone who might be interested, that he was in the big money. It was also arranged that he was to get Rex Turnbull to defend him.

It was on an afternoon when they were leaving Manton's office after one of these planning sessions that Cordari turned to Swift and said:

'You know, Kevin, if we really want to find out about Mendolia we ought to plant someone right on him. At the moment we only get bits of information via informants, who are all people way outside his life merely picking up and passing on odd scraps which are at best second and third hand.'

Swift shot his companion a sidelong glance as they walked together down the corridor.

'What do you have in mind?' he asked.

'Mendolia's a notorious womanizer and I don't see why we shouldn't try to supply him with a new girl-friend. The turn-over rate is pretty high, from all accounts, and all we've got to do is put our candidate where he's bound to notice her.'

'Rather like recommending a victim for an Old Testament sacrifice, isn't it?'

'Not if you choose the right person.'

'Who do you suggest?'

'My sister-in-law,' said Cordari coolly.

Swift gaped at him. 'Are you serious?'

'Absolutely. She's just the girl for the job. She's a reasonable good-looker and she has an insatiable craving for excitement. Heaven knows how many different things she hasn't tried her hand at since she left school. But she's always throwing them up because life gets dull. Why, only yesterday she asked me about joining the police, and actually she'd be jolly good if they didn't keep her in an office, but gave her a bit of cloak-and-dagger stuff to do.'

'How old is she?'

'Twenty-five, I think. I know she's a year or two older than my wife.'

'And not married, I gather?'

'Nope. But not exactly an innocent.'

'And you think we could plant her as Mendolia's next girl?'

'We could have a darned good try.'

'If she agrees.'

'Yes, if she agrees. But knowing Pamela, my bet is she'll jump at it.'

When they left the Yard that evening, Swift accompanied Cordari home.

Pamela Stoughton shared a small flat with a girl-friend about a mile from where the Cordaris lived in Wimbledon, and they decided to call there on their way. As they approached the place, Swift, whose manner had been getting increasingly worried, slowed down.

'Look, Roy, there's the hell of a difference between knocking around with a run of boy-friends and becoming a gangster's mistress. All the difference, in fact, between the enthusiastic amateur and the professional. Are you quite sure this is a good idea?'

'If Pamela doesn't want to play, nothing we can say will make her,' Cordari said. 'Whether or not she becomes his mistress will be her concern. She's able to look after herself all right. It won't be the first time she's coped with a predatory male. Anyway, don't worry; no harm in mentioning it and seeing how she reacts.'

Swift smiled wryly and gave a faint shrug. For the present there was nothing he could do except reserve judgment.

They arrived at the house and climbed three flights of stairs to the top flat. Cordari pressed the bell and a voice at once shouted:

'Hold it a tick, I've got no clothes on.'

'Come as you are; it's only the police,' Cordari called back through the letter-box.

'Why, Roy, what a pleasant surprise,' Pamela Stoughton said, opening the door a moment later. She was wearing a full-length house-coat with the minimum number of buttons done up, and her hair was falling loosely around her shoulders. Swift decided it was pretty hair; perhaps even her best feature. She was on the tall side, though well proportioned, and, in brief, looking pleasingly feminine. She now peered past her brother-in-law. 'And you've brought a handsome visitor, too.'

'Meet Kevin Swift. He's also at the Yard,' Cordari said. She and Swift shook hands. 'Well, come on in and have a drink.'

'That's what we came for.'

'But didn't think to bring a bottle of anything with you, I suppose? No, well, that restricts your choice to beer or something labelled sherry type.'

As soon as they'd got their drinks and sat down, Cordari explained the object of their visit. He was careful, however, to make no mention of his own or Swift's real roles in the matter. He just said it was thought that Mendolia *might* be the boss of a racket to smuggle wanted men out of the country and that ...

well it would be too wonderful if Pamela felt like helping . . . though, of course, it was entirely up to her, as there might be risks attached, and it was all highly unorthodox, so . . . Long before Cordari had finished speaking, Swift knew what her reply was going to be.

'Couldn't be better,' she said when he'd given her an edited account of things. 'Saves me going along to the Labour Exchange.'

'Aren't you still working at that dress shop?'

'Got the sack today. I was rude to a customer—*the* customer . . . a dripping dowager . . . the old bitch!'

'You're hopeless, Pamela,' Cordari said with obvious pride. 'Anyway, since you're game, we'd now better think of ways of palming you off on Mendolia.'

'Leave it to me to do some quiet reconnoitring first. I'd like to find out something about his current tastes.'

'How'll you do that?' Swift asked.

She looked at him in surprise.

'Much the same way as you people discover these things. I've not worked in a couple of shady night clubs without learning a trick or two.'

Cordari gave Swift an amused, what-did-I-tell-you look and got up.

'By the way, I'm afraid this isn't a very well-paid job, my pet,' he said.

'Is it paid at all?'

'No. We can probably tide you over a few days, but not more.'

'If Joe Mendolia's girl-friends want for anything,' she said crisply, after a moment's silence, 'they probably deserve to.'

After leaving Pamela they walked on to Cordari's home, which was about half a mile away. It was a small, new semi-detached house, neat and unoriginal in appearance. As he turned his key and pushed open the front door, Cordari called out:

'Back, darling.'

'Just coming.' The voice came from the kitchen and was accompanied by sounds of pots clattering and a tap being turned on.

A few seconds later Doreen Cordari appeared. She was much smaller than her sister and wore a quiet, almost diffident air.

15

'This is Kevin Swift, darling.'

'Do come in, Mr. Swift. I'll have supper ready soon.'

'I'm sure he'll like it better if you call him Kevin.' Swift nodded. 'Juliet asleep yet?'

'She should be.'

'You look after Kevin while I go and take a peep at her.'

Swift followed Doreen Cordari into the front living-room as Cordari disappeared upstairs.

'Roy hasn't yet got over our new toy,' she said with a shy smile as she motioned Swift to a chair. 'He and Juliet spend hours cooing and gurgling at each other. He's awfully good with her, too. It's amazing the way men nowadays hurl themselves into nappy-changing and all the rest of it.'

'Equality of the sexes,' Swift observed with a grin. 'Husbands pot the baby while their wives go off and mind great hunking pieces of machinery in the factories.'

'Yes, it has almost come to that.' Her expression was thoughtful and Swift watched her with quiet amusement. 'Not that I ever wanted it that way round.' Looking up suddenly and meeting his eyes, she added: 'You've met my sister, Pamela, haven't you?'

'Yes, we called there on our way, this evening.'

'Now, there's someone who'd get along famously in a tough, sex-equality world, though admittedly not doing anything as tedious as minding machinery. To Pamela, God was really being rather capricious when He constructed the sexes differently.'

'Nevertheless, I'm awfully glad He did.'

'Oh, don't misunderstand me; so is Pamela, bless her!'

'Juliet's asleep now,' Cordari said, at that moment coming into the room. 'I believe she'd stayed specially awake to say good night to me.' He perched himself on the side of his wife's chair and, putting an arm round her shoulders, pulled her towards him. To Swift, bachelor and fancy free, it was an agreeable piece of domesticity.

'Now you look after Kevin while I go and dish up,' Doreen said, jumping to her feet.

With a wistful expression, Cordari watched her leave the room. Then he turned back to Swift.

'I can thoroughly recommend marriage to you, Kevin.'

'I must think about it some time.' The words were spoken flippantly, for Swift always affected to prize his liberty too much to accord the idea any serious consideration. One day, doubtless, he would get married; but there was time enough. . . .

On taking his leave of the Cordaris some hours later, however, he found himself walking down the road in a strangely contemplative mood.

CHAPTER FIVE

The third Tuesday in April was the day selected for Rafaele Skourasi's first appearance at West End Magistrates' Court. He was 'arrested' by Detective Sergeant Talper at half past six that morning and brought to the police station, where he was ritually charged with possessing a quantity of Indian Hemp, which had come in fact from a recently seized consignment and which the Metropolitan Police Laboratory had under examination at the time. When he was searched at the station by Talper in the presence of an unsuspecting uniformed sergeant, there was found on him nearly two hundred pounds in cash. 'You're in a profitable line of business, aren't you, son?' Sergeant Talper said. 'Been at it a long time?' Skourasi looked suitably anxious, but said nothing.

During the two weeks in which he had been that character, Cordari had spent most of his days and quite a few of his nights lounging around small cafés and restaurants in Soho, keeping his eyes and ears wide open. He had, however, learnt nothing of any value to the investigation. On the occasions when he himself had discreetly led out the subject of the disappearances, his audiences's reaction had been disappointingly negative. He guessed this was because they either genuinely knew nothing, or, if they did, knew better than to talk about it. The gang leaders were reputed to have long ears and there were some subjects it wasn't wise to know too much about. For all that, Rafaele Skourasi let drop the hint on a number of occasions that should he ever find himself in trouble with the police, he'd be buying a one-way ticket just as soon as he could.

Although his Soho sojourn was apparently fruitless from the point of view of the investigation, he did pick up certain scraps of information which led the police to a cache of stolen jewellery, and, another time enabled them to arrange a handsome reception for a gang of country-house burglars.

17

At ten o'clock on the Tuesday in question, Detective Sergeant Talper arrived at West End Court with his prisoner.

'You sit there, son,' he said, nodding at a bench against the wall in the jailer's office.

Cordari did so, holding his head in his hands and looking a picture of dejection. His heart now started to beat faster as he contemplated what might lie ahead. It was like waiting for the starters pistol in a track race, with the further excitement of not being able to see the finishing post, or yet of knowing whether or not the start would be a false one.

He looked across at Sergeant Talper, who was talking to P.C. Tredgold, the jailer. Tredgold was going through the day's charge sheets, on which among other things were listed the prisoners' possessions on arrest. When his eye caught the sum of '£186' on Skourasi's sheet, he looked up sharply in Cordari's direction and made a muttered comment to Talper, who chuckled.

'Cheer up,' said a kindly voice suddenly. Cordari raised his head to find Plowman, the usher, towering over him. 'I always say you never know your luck. There's no point in giving up hope until you actually find yourself being wheeled away in the Black Maria.'

Cordari smiled wanly, uncertain how to react to this well-meant encouragement. Plowman was a brawny fellow with warm, friendly eyes, and Cordari couldn't help reflecting that he'd have looked better in policeman's blue than in the ridiculously skimpy black gown he wore as an usher. It had presumably been handed down to him by a predecessor in office, who had been half his size.

'Lord Droxford's fair enough,' Plowman continued. 'He'll treat you O.K. He's not anti-foreigner or anything of that sort. Just as well, too, in this court, seeing that a good many of our customers have unpronounceable names.'

'Hey, Arnold,' P.C. Tredgold called out. 'Sergeant Talper wants to have a word with Mr. Astbury. Is he in yet?'

Plowman looked up at the large clock on the wall.

'Yes, he's in,' he replied without hesitation. 'Always arrives on the tick of a quarter past ten.' He drifted over to that side of the office, and Sergeant Talper made to go in search of the clerk.

'Keep an eye on him,' he said to P.C. Tredgold over his shoulder, nodding in Cordari's direction.

'Well, how are things with you this morning, Arnold?' Tredgold asked heartily as Plowman leaned comfortably on the counter.

'No so dusty, Albert, except for the wife.'

'She still playing you up?'

Plowman made a despairing noise.

'Nothing's ever right for her. You'd think she lived on a diet of acid drops.'

Tredgold shook his head in sympathetic understanding.

'They can be real pips, can't they? Now, take my brother's wife . . .'

Cordari removed his mind from the domestic troubles of Plowman and P.C. Tredgold's brother, and thought about his own wife, who was to him the most adorable thing in life. For a fleeting second he had an overwhelming urge to cry halt to the whole plan and run home.

Sergeant Talper knocked on Mr. Astbury's door and entered.

'Good morning, Sergeant. What can I do for you?'

'It's about a case I have here today, sir—a man called Skourasi who's charged with an offence under the Dangerous Drugs Act. I thought I ought to explain, sir, that I shan't be opposing bail, since the police believe he's likely to lead us onto something much bigger if he's let out.'

'And why are you telling me this?'

'I wondered whether you'd think it wise to tip off Lord Droxford, sir. Ordinarily, of course, we'd oppose bail, and the magistrate may wonder why we're not doing so in this case.'

'Isn't it a bit of a risk bailing him?' Sergeant Talper pretended not to understand the import of the question, and Mr. Astbury went on: 'It's become, as you're doubtless aware, rather a habit among our defendants not to answer to their bail.'

'Oh, that, sir! I'm sure my superiors have taken that fully into account in deciding not to oppose it in this case.'

Mr. Astbury, who somewhat resembled a benign schoolmaster, now looked at Sergeant Talper over the top of his spectacles.

'Right, Sergeant,' he said, 'I'll mention it.'

It was one of West End's lighter days, and Cordari's case was called immediately after the usual procession of prostitutes, who had come to pay their morning tribute to the Revenue following their night's work.

P.C. Tredgold bustled him into the dock and announced:

'Charge number twelve, sir. Rafaele Skourasi.'

19

At this, Sergeant Talper stepped nimbly into the witness-box.
'This man was arrested only this morning, sir, and I ask for a formal remand for seven days.'

Lord Droxford, who had been studying the charge in his register, now looked first at Cordari, then at Sergeant Talper.

'Do you object to bail, Sergeant?'

'No, sir, not with suitable conditions, and if the accused surrenders his passport.'

'Tell me, first, how much of this hemp did he have in his possession?'

'Only about an ounce, sir.'

Lord Droxford pursed his lips and frowned.

'*Only?* But that's quite a sizeable amount in concentrated form.'

'Yes, sir,' Sergeant Talper agreed meekly. It seemed that the magistrate was going to be tricky about bail after all, and he sent up a hasty prayer as he glanced quickly at Cordari, who was standing impassively in the dock. He also caught sight of Swift among the throng of spectators at the back of the court.

'If I do decide to grant him bail, can he find acceptable sureties?' Lord Droxford asked after an agonizing pause.

'I understand so, sir,' Talper replied encouragingly. This was better, for the plan included the presence in court of two persons primed for this service if required.

'All right,' Lord Droxford said, with apparent reluctance, after another pause. 'Skourasi, you can have bail on your own recognizance of one hundred pounds and with two sureties each in a like amount.'

The bail formalities completed, Cordari was remanded to appear again a week hence. As Tredgold motioned him to leave the dock, he gripped the rail in front of him and said in carefully accented tones.

'I'd like legal aid, if you please.'

Mr. Astbury looked up as though stung by a bee, and seizing the charge sheet turned to Lord Droxford and announced: 'This man had over one hundred and eighty pounds on him when he was arrested, sir.'

It was Lord Droxford's turn to look startled.

'Certainly not,' he snapped at the prisoner. 'You can well afford to pay for a lawyer. I've seldom heard such an impudent application.'

During this exchange, Rex Turnbull, the solicitor, who'd just come into court, swung round quickly to get a better look at a potential client and also to ensure the converse. But Cordari had recognized a certain menace in the magistrate's tone and hastened out of court before the decision to grant him bail could be reconsidered.

Ten minutes later he stood on the pavement outside the courthouse listening to old Susannah's music while he gazed thoughtfully at the entrance to Rex Turnbull's offices.

Once or twice, aware that someone was close beside her, the old Negress looked with unseeing eyes in his direction, and eventually he dropped sixpence into her tin. Then with sudden decision he went across the street and disappeared into the building.

A few minutes later he was out on the pavement once more, having paid a deposit of fifty pounds and been given an appointment to see Rex Turnbull at four that afternoon.

As he walked back to his room above the tailor's shop he wondered how soon it would be before the other side made a move. Now that the plan proper had been launched, it never occurred to him to think in terms of 'if'; only 'when'.

Swift's thoughts were similar as he slowly sipped at a cup of strong coffee in the bar which stood across the road from the tailor's shop.

CHAPTER SIX

The six days that followed were as mentally enervating as any Cordari could remember. Optimism and excitement slowly waned and gave way to frustration and a sense of anti-climactic let-down.

As he wandered about the streets of Soho, waiting for something to happen, he daily became gloomier. Much of the time he spent going the rounds of every possible place where he thought contact might be made, in the course of which he consumed enough coffee and salami rolls to feed a hungry nation.

The room which he had rented was above the shop of a tailor named Mustapha. It was bare and uninviting, and Cordari was never so sharply reminded of his own small but cosy home as when he returned to the room each evening.

Mustapha, a hard-working, morose man, kept himself to himself and appeared to expect others to do likewise. All Cordari's efforts to get to know him had been foredoomed to dismal failure. Of a Mrs. Mustapha there was now no sign, though Cordari gathered that the tailor's girl assistant was, in fact, also his daughter. She looked about sixteen and had the largest pair of eyes Cordari had ever seen. She used to watch him covertly as he went in and out of the building, and at one time he thought she might be doing so on her father's instructions. But subsequently her hasty withdrawal, on a number of occasions, at the first sound of a paternal bark from the interior of the shop caused him to revise this opinion. Only once had Cordari attempted to speak to her and then her sole response had been to stare him out of countenance before turning away and disappearing into a room at the back. There was something primitive about her which made an anomaly of her presence in the heart of London.

There were two other tenants in the house beside Cordari. One was Lil, a prostitute from Leicester: the other a youth with a narrow, vicious face whom Cordari suspected of being a deserter from the Forces. At all events, he appeared to do no work and was usually to be seen in one of the shabbier cafés of the district.

'I don't like talking to strangers,' he had said when Cordari had tried to get into conversation with him; and there had been something cold and reptilian about his eyes when he spoke. Cordari had always held the view that the eyes mirrored the soul more clearly than any other physical feature, and in this instance had not been enchanted by what he saw.

But to make up for Mustapha's dourness and the young man of surly disposition, there was always Leicester Lil, and a warm bond of companionship quickly developed between her and Cordari. When not industriously plying her trade, she was always ready to sit and chat. Morever, she was a sympathetic listener to whom Cordari, to his own surprise, several times found himself talking about his wife and baby daughter. This he was encouraged to do, since it was part of their relationship that neither ever attempted to probe beyond what the other said. To have done so would also have offended against local convention, Soho's lonely lodgers knowing better than to be overtly inquisitive about each other. Ask no questions and you'll be told no lies had a special application within its purlieus.

It was one evening when he was thoroughly tired and felt his morale was in particular danger of buckling that he found himself in one of Mendolia's clubs. This was *The Pink Oracle*, which he had visited before (he'd made a special point of joining all Mendolia's clubs) and which had struck him as being like all the rest, namely dark, expensive, noisy, suffocating and dull. Indeed, one of Cordari's disillusionments had been to discover that Soho had somehow lost the panache he'd always associated with it. True, it still abounded with pimps and prostitutes, and with perverts of both sexes. True again there were few vices that couldn't be practised once you knew the open sesame to the haunts which catered for their addicts, whether gambling, drug or sex. But outwardly it was all quite respectable and rather colourless. Maybe the siting, in its very midst, of a huge police section house, where a veritable army of officers lived, had had the same chastening effect as would the presence of the headmaster sleeping in the Lower III's dormitory. Doubtless the inquisitive innocent at large could still run into trouble in Soho, but he'd have to ask pretty hard for it, as by waving his wallet about in one of the drab and disreputable cafés frequented by coloured men, who were liable to get hemped up with an evening's progress.

On this particular evening, Cordari had allowed himself to succumb to the blandishments of the blonde whom *The Pink Oracle* employed as commissionaire to lure in new customers. Dressed rather like a circus ring-master, she stood just inside the doorway of the premises, projecting her appeal at passers-by.

The small bar downstairs was empty except for a middle-aged man with balding head and faded melancholy eyes who was sitting in a corner, whispering to a sharp-faced and bored-looking youth. In the room which led off the bar, another pansy was playing softly on the piano and a couple of toughies (Cordari had noticed them on his previous visits, too) lounged at a table. At the far side of this room was a closely guarded door which, Cordari guessed from the traffic that passed through it, led to gambling tables.

He nodded at the barman and ordered a Scotch, and then another. By the time he reached his fourth, the place was filling up. The blonde commissionaire upstairs was clearly in good magnetic form this evening.

It was not so much the words as the voice that caused him suddenly to turn his moody gaze along the bar.

23

'I'd love a champagne cocktail.'

Pamela Stoughton and Joe Mendolia were easing themselves on to a couple of stools at the opposite end from him.

'Make it two,' Mendolia added to the barman.

'Yes, Mr. Mendolia,' the barman said, springing into unaccustomed action. Indeed, the owner's presence was having an electric effect all round, for even the two toughs in the other room sauntered through and made pointed efforts to ingratiate themselves. They were, however, quickly sent back to their posts.

'We won't stay here long. It's just that I make a point of dropping in at my places unannounced from time to time. It keeps everyone on their toes.' As he spoke, Mendolia's gaze went round the bar, like that of a Roman emperor. He picked up his glass and his features broke into an engaging grin as he toasted Pamela. 'Let this be the first of many.' When he lowered his glass, he went on: 'I'm going to take you somewhere to dinner where you'll get the best food in Town. And I don't mean equal best. I mean *the* best.'

'Where's that?' Pamela asked enthusiastically.

'My flat.'

'I might have guessed,' she said with a giggle.

After about twenty minutes they got up and departed. Just before they did so, Mendolia left Pamela's side and went through the door which led to the presumably more money-making part of the establishment. He was away for two or three minutes, and during this time Cordari and Pamela sat at their respective stools without exchanging so much as a glimmer of recognition. Only a long training in self-discipline enabled Cordari to do this, since it was the first indication he had had that Pamela had made first base and he itched to know more.

Fairly soon after she and Mendolia had gone, he also left, giving the commissionaire's behind a friendly slap by way of farewell. A shadowy figure detached itself from an opposite doorway and followed him. Round the corner Cordari stopped and the figure came up to him.

'See them, Kevin?' Cordari asked.

Swift nodded. 'Yep. Arrived and departed in a chauffeur-driven Rolls Bentley. Anything happened yet?'

'Not a rustle. Maybe I've overplayed the part or something. There can't now be many people in Soho who *haven't* seen my roll of bank-notes. I'm almost surprised I've not been cracked over the head and robbed.' His tone was gloom itself. 'Any idea what Mr. Manton has in mind if nothing's happened by the day after tomorrow when I appear in court again.'

'There's a conference tomorrow afternoon to consider what to do.'

'It could be, I suppose, that the organization has been disbanded,' Cordari said, in a still-dejected tone.

'Could be anything,' Swift replied unhelpfully. 'At least, Roy, you're not standing about in draughty doorways all the time. Why, you're actually drinking Scotch at the Government's expense. Not to mention having a prospective free trip to North Africa.'

Cordari smiled weakly and the two men parted, Cordari to his room above the tailor's shop and Swift to his temporary bed at the nearby section house in Broadwick Street.

On the morning that he was due to reappear in court, Cordari had just finished washing and shaving when a sound over by the door attracted his attention. He turned his head and saw that a letter was lying on the floor. For a full minute he stared at it without moving, for it was the first mail he'd received in his three-week sojourn there. Then with heart beating faster he walked over and picked it up.

It was addressed in block capitals to 'Mr. Rafaele Skourasi' and bore a 'London, W.1' postmark, of 5.30 p.m. the previous day. This much Cordari took in before opening it.

Inside was a folded half-sheet of paper, on which instructions were printed in neat, pencilled capitals. It read:

IF YOU'RE INTERESTED IN AVOIDING GOING TO PRISON, FOLLOW THESE INSTRUCTIONS CAREFULLY. WHEN YOU LEAVE COURT TOMORROW DROP ONE THREEPENNY BIT AND ONE HALFPENNY SEPARATELY INTO SUSANNAH'S TIN: THEN AWAIT FURTHER INSTRUCTIONS. FOR YOUR OWN GOOD YOU SHOULD NOT DISCUSS THIS WITH ANYONE AS IT WILL RUIN YOUR CHANCES OF A SAFE GETAWAY. IT'S UP TO YOU.

Cordari read it through a second and a third time. His mouth felt dry and his stomach full of butterflies.

So there was to be a zero hour after all.

25

CHAPTER SEVEN

At the time, it didn't occur to him that the last-minute nature of the message might be intentional. Later he was able to see this as part of the care taken by the mysterious other side to forestall detection. But all he could think of now was the near-impossibility of passing the news on to Swift in time for the next phase of the plan to be put into operation. He hadn't a moment to waste.

When, an hour and a half later, he arrived at court, he found Susannah had beaten him to it. There was nothing unusual in this, since she made a point of getting there soon after half past nine each morning, having discovered that people were inclined to be more generous when they arrived than when they left. This applied particularly to defendants, who appeared to nourish the hope that a simple act of charity would be instantly noted on high and communicated to Lord Droxford before he came to deal with their case. It was a cosy superstition that harmed no one.

Susannah was playing and singing an old spiritual when Cordari approached. Her voice was deep and throaty, her expression as impassive as ever.

But today he saw her through new eyes. She represented something faintly sinister, and it was all he could do to assail her with a torrent of urgent questions.

Inside the court building, everything was exactly the same. Defendants would come and defendants would go, but West End Court would go on for ever—or so it seemed.

As Cordari passed through the main hall, Mr. Turnbull's chief clerk button-holed him.

' 'Morning, Mr. Skourasi. Mr. Turnbull wants to have a word with you. He's in the interview room now, so I'll take you to him.'

Cordari followed him to a cell-like room where it was possible for lawyers to have a more or less private word with their clients.

'Ah, good morning, Mr. Skourasi,' Mr. Turnbull began as soon as Cordari had been shown in. 'I fear I have some rather tiresome news for you. The police are going to ask for a further remand. They say they're not yet ready to go ahead with the case. Now how do you feel about it?' Before Cordari could answer he went on: 'Of course I intend to protest about the delay. It's a good thing to shake the police up about that, even though it may really suit us quite well.'

Cordari stated he had no objection, and silently supposed that Mr. Turnbull's clients were not the sort who took kindly to any suggestion of collaboration with the police.

'That's fine, then, Mr. Skourasi. By the way, there is just one other thing. Perhaps you could slip across to my office afterwards—only for a moment. One or two little formalities to be attended to.'

Cordari guessed that this was a euphemistic reference to a coming request for more money. For devilment, he put his hand in his pocket and pulled out a fat roll of bank-notes. Mr. Turnbull looked pinkly embarrassed.

'No. No, Mr. Skourasi. Not now,' he said hastily.

They emerged from the interview room and went into the jailer's office.

'You here again already?' Plowman cheerfully greeted Cordari. 'Then it must be Tuesday. Always tell the day of the week by defendants' faces,' he explained. 'Your face'll mean Tuesday till we get rid of you. Lot to be said for this business of remanding people for a week at a time. Hardly ever need a calendar. I remember one time soon after I came here a year or two back, there was an old chap whose case must have gone on every Friday for nigh on a couple of months. Friday after it finished I didn't know where I was; just couldn't think where we'd got to in the week. Funny old world when you get to that state, isn't it?'

Cordari agreed that it was indeed, and Plowman moved off to cheer up someone else with his recollections.

When at last P.C. Tredgold called out 'Rafaele Skourasi' and escorted Cordari into court, the morning was well on. His own occupancy of the dock this time, however, was brief.

Sergeant Talper asked for the further remand, Mr Turnbull protested without opposing and Lord Droxford, barely looking in Cordari's direction, put the case over to the following Tuesday. Mr. Astbury neither spoke nor looked up.

A few minutes later, clutching a threepenny bit and a halfpenny so that they almost melted in his hand, Cordari stepped out on to the pavement. The scene, as he glanced quickly about him, could not have looked more normal, and yet in approximately fifteen seconds' time he would be taking an irrevocable step into the dark unknown. Carefully and deliberately he dropped the two coins into Susannah's tin one after the other and unconsciously braced himself for something to happen. But not only was there no magical puff of smoke or sudden dissolution of the world about him, but Susannah herself appeared not to take any notice other than to pick out the money and quickly secrete it in her coat pocket.

Disillusioned, Cordari walked slowly past her and on back to the sanctuary of his room.

From his position across the street, Swift had kept watch, also waiting for something dramatic to happen. But there'd been nothing. Susannah hadn't moved, and had continued to sing and play with no more than her customary pauses between numbers. Moreover, not a soul had either approached her or spoken to her. When one o'clock came and she packed up, Swift followed her. Just before two she returned to her pitch. By then Swift had found out that she occupied a room in a house in Sirena Street about a quarter of a mile away, living alone, looking after herself and apparently having truck with no one.

For the rest of that day, while Cordari never strayed far from his room, Swift kept a ceaseless watch first on Susannah herself till she went home and then on the house where she lived.

But still nothing happened, and about eleven o'clock, when he'd satisfied himself that she had retired for the night, he stole away.

As he walked slowly back to the section house he found his thoughts centring on Pamela. Come to think of it, they'd been drifting there with increasing frequency of late. The fact that he hadn't seen her to speak to for over a week (and in fact had only done so at all on two occasions) had done nothing to relegate her in his mind.

It had been arranged between the three of them that she shouldn't try to get in touch with himself or Cordari unless she had something important to report.

A slight pang now went through Swift as he thought of her with Mendolia. He was sure it couldn't be jealousy, since he hardly knew her, and you couldn't be jealous of someone you'd only twice spoken to. But the fact did remain he'd never previously met anyone who had crept so insistently into his thoughts.

He was in a wistful, giving way to a disgruntled, frame of mind by the time he turned into the doorway of the monastic establishment within whose walls strict celibacy was enjoined.

Though the remainder of that day had brought nothing fresh, events had nevertheless started to move. It was therefore with no surprise that on the following morning Cordari saw another letter slipped beneath his door. Indeed, he was half watching for it.

It was addressed in the same way as the previous one, though the postmark, this time, was 'London, S.E.1.' It was clearly not intended that any conclusions should be drawn from the mailing of letters in the same postal district.

Envelope, paper and writing were all the same as before. Only the text of the message was different. It read:

EVERYTHNG ARRANGED FOR YOUR JOURNEY. BE IN PUBLIC TELEPHONE BOX NEAR THE NORTH-EAST CORNER OF GOLDEN SQUARE AT ELEVEN TONIGHT AND READY FOR IMMEDIATE MOVE. HAVE £500 IN £1 NOTES. NO TRICKS MIND OR YOU'LL BE THE ONE WHO COMES OFF BADLY. ASSURING YOU OF A SAFE TRIP AND THE BEST ATTENTION AT ALL TIMES.

'Looks as though we're not going to have much time,' Manton said to Swift as they sat discussing matters together in his office at the Yard. 'It's pretty obvious that when Cordari gets that call tonight he'll be told where to go, and there'll be no question of packing a bag and saying a round of good-byes.'

'No, sir, but I'll be waiting outside and he'll have time to pass me the dope before he's off.'

'Don't be too obviously hanging about that telephone box. For all we know, it's been chosen because they have it under observation themselves.'

'Perhaps we should get the exchange, sir, to trace the number from which they make their call.'

'Hardly worth it, even if it's possible. It's certain to be from another public call-box which'll tell us nothing.'

'What do you make of the threat at the end of the note, sir?'

'I guess it's just a way of warning the chap not to go opening his mouth too wide.'

'But what could they do, even if he did?'

Manton shook his head. 'If anything were to put them on their guard, presumably the whole thing would be called off. I

29

can't see that they'd be able to take reprisals, but—but—well, we just don't know what they might try to do. The note strikes me as being a crude mixture of assurance and warning against indiscretion.' He scanned the eager young face on the other side of his desk. 'So far you've had the dull end of the job, but this evening yours is going to be the vital role. Everything depends on your seeing exactly where Cordari is taken and what happens to him—without the opposition spotting you.'

'Yes, I appreciate that, sir. Roy and I have got a fairly good system of signals worked out, and I think we should be able to keep in touch without arousing any suspicions.'

Manton, however, looked dubious, and said:

'I hope you will be able to; but from moves that have already been made, they're a crafty lot, and I'll be surprised if the next stage—that of actual contact—hasn't been planned to avoid every possibility of detection. Remember, if anything does go wrong or you do lose contact, get on to me immediately.'

'Yes, I promise I'll do that, sir.'

'And don't forget that if it's a question of following him anywhere, there'll be a cab with one of our chaps at the wheel parked round the corner from the call-box.' Swift nodded and grinned. He knew that though the vehicle in question might have a slightly antique air, beneath its bonnet was an engine which liked nothing better than to test itself against Mercedes, Aston Martins and the lot.

An officer knocked on the door and came in. He handed Manton a sealed envelope.

'Detective Sergeant Talper told me to give you this, sir,' he said, and left again, glancing curiously at Swift.

'Let's just see what's in this before you go,' Manton said.

He slit the envelope open with a finger and took out a single sheet of paper. Swift watched him read it and observed that his expression became heavily pensive. It was some moments before he spoke, and when he did his voice made no betrayal of his thoughts.

'We've done another check on the friends and relations of our six fugitives. This is the result. Apart from receiving the initial letters from Algeria, it's confirmed that none of them has heard a thing.' He chewed nervously at the corner of his mouth, then shook himself and gave Swift a wry smile. 'Wish Cordari luck from me; I think he's going to need it. I think you both are.'

CHAPTER EIGHT

As Cordari took a final glance round his room—the room which had been his home these past three weeks—he was swept by a feeling of unutterable melancholy. For the first time the hard iron bedstead looked almost comfortable. There was something friendly, too, about the chipped basin and water-jug on the marble wash-stand over in the corner. And the fly-blown picture of the dimpled shepherdess gazing placidly at six skipping lambs now made him think unaccountably of Doreen and their baby daughter.

He opened the door and shut it quickly behind him with an air of irrevocability. Looking at his watch, he saw that it was eighteen minutes to eleven. Time to go, and yet he felt suddenly constrained by the unreality of his impending journey, and paralysed by a reluctance to embark upon it.

The mood passed. He moved to the top of the stairs and was about to descend when the front door opened and two people entered and started to come up. He stood aside to let them pass. They were Leicester Lil and one of her gentlemen clients. In the course of his three-week sojourn, Cordari had seen Lil with a great number of different men and had come to enjoy the short snatches of conversation he and she invariably exchanged when they met on the stairs. She was the proverbially golden-hearted prostitute and had a friendly word for everyone, except the Metropolitan Police, on whom she poured streams of caustic abuse, much to Cordari's secret amusement.

'Hello, ducks,' she said as she reached the top of the stairs and saw him. 'You just off on the prowl again?' Cordari nodded and gave her a wink, his gaze shifting to the small perspiring but determined-looking man just behind her. 'Yes, I get 'em in all sizes,' she added in a whisky whisper as she passed him to go on up to her room.

Cordari went downstairs, feeling curiously better. At the bottom he saw a light shining through the partially open door at the back of the premises. This was the room in which Mustapha, the tailor, did most of his work, and where he kept the huge irons with which he pressed the completed garments. Its atmosphere was always a fascinating blend of stale steam and garlic, to which the irons and Mustapha made their respective contributions.

31

By the time Cordari got out on to the pavement, it was twelve minutes to eleven. He crossed the street and had a quick look inside the café where he'd recently been spending so much time. Toni, the proprietor, was at the far end of the counter reading an evening paper and picking industriously at his teeth. Otherwise, it was almost empty, and he was able to account for the few who were in there. With a last look at the large bloodless ham which adorned the window, surrounded by mounds of chocolate wafers and other ill-assorted wares, he set off for the telephone kiosk.

There were few people about, and none of them, anyway, appeared to have the slightest interest in him. The evening was a warm one and to Cordari it seemed oppressively so.

He decided to go by a route which would enable him to observe the call-box some hundred yards or so before he actually reached it. Straining his eyes as soon as it came into sight he could see that it was presently unoccupied. But now he was seized by a new anxiety. What if someone should slip in ahead of him and take the call meant for him? Should he then wait in the hope that his contact would try again? That would presumably depend on whether the contact realized the wrong person had answered in the first place. Anyhow, he, Cordari, couldn't very well tackle anyone who might receive the call in error. Of course, if it were a woman, the contact would know at once something had gone amiss. But would he realize what?

Even while these thoughts were chasing through his head, he reached the telephone kiosk and stepped inside, letting the door swing to behind him. There was the usual acrid smell of stale cigarette smoke and it was infernally hot.

He'd hardly time to think further when the bell suddenly rang. He started violently, but immediately lifted the receiver.

'Hello?' he said in a nervous tone.

'Skourasi?'

'Yes.'

'All ready?'

'Yes.'

'Got the money?'

'Yes.'

'How much?'

'Five hundred like you said.'

'Good. At half past eleven walk along Derry Street. Go from west to east and stay on the north pavement. Pretend to be

32

drunk and stagger about; but don't overdo it. That's all. Everything clear?'

'Yes.'

For answer there was a metallic click as the person at the other end rang off.

The voice had been a man's, and that was all Cordari could say. It had been a voice devoid of all idiosyncrasy or of any memorable quality.

It was now that he fully appreciated for the first time with what care and cunning the enemy executed each move.

Certain that he wasn't being followed, but nevertheless weaving his way through an alley and doubling back down another just in case, he came to where Swift was waiting for him. Quickly he told him what had happened. When he finished, Swift glanced at his watch.

'It's ten past eleven now. We've only got twenty minutes.'

'I know.'

'And Derry Street! They would choose there. It's miserably lit and all the doorways are flush on the pavement. There isn't a decent observation post in the whole street.'

'Obviously that's why it's been selected.'

'O.K., Roy, I'd better skip along there now. If you give me a ten-minute start you should be there just on time.' In a reflective tone, he went on: 'I could possibly get myself into a window in one of the houses, but it's running things a bit fine; and anyway, even though I could see, I wouldn't be able to act quickly if the need arose. No, I think my best bet is to take our cab up there and have it innocently parked at some vantage-point.'

'Yep, that's a good idea, Kevin. You'll be able to see without being seen and it'll be easy to hop out if necessary.'

'Right, Roy. I'm off.' Swift thrust out his hand. 'Best of luck—and think of that medal you're going to get.'

Cordari gripped the outstretched hand.

'Thanks,' he said. 'And as for the medal, I might even think of lending it to you occasionally.'

Swift later reckoned that he packed more physical and mental activity into the next twelve minutes than he normally did into the same number of days. At the end of that period of time, he was sitting on the floor of the cab which was parked at the west end of Derry Street and on its south side. Being also just round

33

the corner from a small night club, he hoped it would appear that it had come to pick up someone from there. But if anyone should look inside and see an apparently inert body on the floor ... Well, that problem would have to take care of itself if and when it arose. He couldn't think of everything in the time at his disposal.

It was now two minutes to the half-hour and he peered cautiously out. As far as he could see, the street was quite empty. It ran straight for about two hundred yards from the end where the cab was parked and connected two of Soho's better-known thoroughfares. Not only was it badly lit and devoid of observation posts, as he had already remarked, but it was joined by a number of narrow alleys of the type that abound in the area and provide a fugitive's paradise.

The sound of scraping shoe leather caused Swift to switch his gaze. There on the far pavement and almost opposite the cab was Cordari. His hands were plunged deep in his raincoat pockets, his head rolling slightly and his mouth was loosely open. He was walking slowly and his gait was just unsteady enough to give an impression of inebriation.

As he wove his way along the pavement and the distance between him and the cab increased, Swift muttered anxious curses to himself. The cab couldn't move now without arousing suspicion, and yet if nothing happened till Cordari reached the far end of the street he wasn't going to be able to see a damn thing.

Already Cordari was almost half-way there and was little more than a floating shadow. What was more, after he passed the next street light on that side, it would be almost impossible to keep an eye on him at all.

Quickly and almost noiselessly Swift opened the near-side door of the cab and slipped out on to the pavement. Then hugging the house-line he moved with a stealth which little betrayed the turmoil of his mind. Cordari was now well over a hundred yards ahead of him, and he decided it was better to risk detection than lose the trail by inaction.

Suddenly from out of the shadows Swift saw a figure materialize. He appeared to put an arm round Cordari and immediately to quicken the pace to a fast walk. A moment later they had both disappeared.

Seized by panic and throwing all caution to the winds, Swift sprinted to the spot where he'd last seen them. It couldn't have

34

taken him much more than twelve seconds and the street seemed to ring with the sound of his flying footsteps. He halted in a pool of darkness between two lights and looked desperately about him. There was a gap between two houses where an alley ran. They could only have gone up it, and Swift did likewise. Some way along it was diagonally intersected by another where a gas lamp on a wall bracket hissed to give a throbbing light. As he stood there wondering which to take, a youth came along whistling.

'Have you seen a couple of men?' Swift asked peremptorily. 'Quick, I must have an answer.'

For reply he got a stream of profanities.

'Cut that out,' he said sharply. 'This is a police matter. It's urgent.'

The youth stared at him insolently for a moment, trying to decide whether or not to believe him.

'No, I ain't,' he said, and spat just to the left of Swift's feet. He had started to move off when Swift grabbed him.

'Look, I want the truth. Are you quite certain you haven't seen two men the way you've just come from?'

'I've told you, 'aven't I?' The youth looked distastefully at Swift's hand holding his shoulder sleeves and shrugged himself free. 'I ain't seen a bleeding soul.' It must have been that Swift's expression of sudden forlorness touched him, for he added half gruffly, half resentfully: 'And that's the truth.'

'O.K.'

Though it was obviously hopeless, Swift quickly reconnoitred each of the alleys that sprouted from the junction. Nowhere, however, was there a sign of Cordari or his mysterious companion, nor yet a clue as to where they might have gone. It could have been through any one of a hundred dark doors: it could even have been right out of the district. Inquiries of several other people, including a patrolling policeman, drew equal blanks.

It was in a spirit of black dejection that he regained the cab and told the driver to take him straight to the Yard.

CHAPTER NINE

Swift's first reaction had been to urge Manton to let him go to the house in Sirena Street and tackle Susannah. Manton had, however, immediately pointed out that this would achieve nothing other than to put the other side on its guard, which was the last thing they wanted to do at this particular moment. Indeed, he had added, there couldn't be a worse moment at which to do it. They had just made their first contact and must now move with the utmost delicacy.

When in the small hours of the morning he returned to a more rational frame of mind, Swift was able to recognize the truth of this argument, though it did little to mitigate his feeling of personal failure.

He spent the night and the whole of the next morning at the Yard waiting for news from Cordari, until finally Manton sent him off for a few hours' rest.

'It doesn't look now as though we're going to hear anything today. From what we know of their earlier moves, it's probable he's already out of the country. They obviously don't believe in unnecessary hanging about, and, anyway, they wouldn't be likely to make final contact until they were ready to transport him.'

'That would mean it all happened during the night, sir, while we were sitting here,' Swift said in a tone of heavy self-reproach.

Manton studied him for a moment without speaking, then he said:

'Just because you were unable to keep in touch with Cordari doesn't mean the whole plan has failed. Far from it. In fact, except for that, everything's gone exactly as we hoped it would. We've got our man into the enemy's camp and with luck we'll soon be hearing from him, even though we may have to exercise a bit of patience. Now you go off and get some rest.'

After a few hours' sleep, Swift awoke refreshed and with one thought uppermost in his mind. That he must see Pamela. He 'phoned her flat (it was about four o'clock in the afternoon) and to his surprise found her in.

After the usual exchange of preliminaries, he said:

'When can I see you? I think we ought to have a chat pretty soon.'

'I think so too. The trouble is——'

'What about this evening?'

'I'm meeting the boy-friend just after seven.'

'What about now?'

'This minute you mean?'

'As soon as I can get out to Wimbledon. In about forty minutes, say?'

'Yes, that would do fine. Is Roy coming too?'

'No, he won't be able to.'

'Oh, well, that means I needn't run out for more beer. I'll just put a couple of bottles in the fridge for you.'

'What about yourself?'

'Don't worry. Mine are already there.'

Swift grinned into the receiver and rang off.

It took slightly less time to get there than he'd expected, but, despite this, the door opened almost before he'd removed his finger from the bell-push.

His expression must have given him away, for Pamela said, 'Yes, nice isn't it?' looking down at the olive green frock she was wearing. It was a crisp, shiny material which, to Swift, looked the ultimate in expense. Moreover, the frock revealed a pair of slender legs which the house-coat of the previous visit had kept from view. He continued to stare and Pamela went on: 'Well, come on in.' She led the way into the living-room. 'Honesty compels me to say I haven't put this lot on for your benefit.' She noticed his gaze fall on her accessories lying on the table. 'I thought we could travel back into Town together.'

'Where are you meeting him?'

'His flat.'

'You're obviously well in,' he said, watching her face intently.

'Yes and no,' she replied, pouring out a glass of ice-cold lager and handing it to him, and then doing the same for herself. 'I've certainly got him interested in me, shall I say, socially, but he shows no inclination to open up about his business activities. He just doesn't seem to be the sort whose girl-friends are *ex officio* confidantes.'

There was something strange about her tone, as though she didn't wish to be pressed on the subject. Nevertheless, Swift began: 'So you haven't been able to discover anything about...'

'About his connections with your smuggling organization? No.'

'But you're sticking at it? You're not backing out, I mean?'

Her eyes suddenly flashed and she seemed on the point of a sharp retort. But the moment passed and she said thoughtfully:

'It matters a lot to you and Roy, my finding out about Mendolia, doesn't it?'

'Yes, as Roy explained——'

She made a gesture of slight impatience and broke in:

'There's more to it than he told me, isn't there? Roy didn't explain everything. But I'm not worrying about that. What you tell me or don't tell me is your concern. But since Roy hasn't been home for nearly three weeks, and makes mysterious 'phone calls to Doreen without telling her where he is or what he's doing, it's pretty obvious you're both up to something out of the ordinary. I say "Both", because all this started soon after he brought you along here and suggested I should get acquainted with Mendolia, and it's clear there's a tie-up.' Swift looked uncomfortable. 'You needn't feel embarrassed; I'm not pumping you. But I've been thinking things over and I'm just telling you a few of the conclusions I've reached since you were last here.' She paused and looked reflectively about the room before returning her gaze to him and saying with decision: 'No, I'm backing out of nothing. I'll do all I can to find out whether Mendolia is linked with your human smuggling racket. Now are you satisfied?'

For answer, Swift put out a hand and gently took one of hers. For a few seconds there was a bond of silent understanding between them, then she said:

'May one ask where Roy is now—or is that secret?'

'It's easily and truthfully answered,' he said with a note of returning bitterness. 'I don't know.'

'I see. Some sort of a secret mission, eh?' He nodded. 'Look, Kevin, will you promise me one thing? Not to bother Doreen with any of this without telling me first. I don't want her to worry about either Roy or me.'

'I promise. You're a very thoughtful person, aren't you?'

'No more than average. But I happen to be very fond of my sister and also of my little brother-in-law, even though he is a policeman.'

They had somehow come closer together on the settee and Swift was now suddenly filled with a strong physical yearning for her. He longed for the momentary oblivion of her embrace, for the temporary dissolution of life's reality. Almost before he had realized what had happened, she had leant forward and kissed him quickly but expertly on the lips.

'And that's to show he's not the only policeman I like,' she said as she jumped to her feet to avoid his hungry follow-up. 'Come on, it's time we went.'

Reluctantly he followed her out of the house. On the way back into Town, it was agreed that he should 'phone her at the flat each day. But he wasn't to worry, she said, if he should sometimes fail to get an answer.

They parted at Victoria Underground station, where Pamela got out to take a cab to Mendolia's flat. Kevin Swift stayed in the train, and for the two stations ride on to Westminster brooded heavily on the question of her relations with Joe Mendolia. As to these, she had, he realized, studiously avoided giving him a single clue.

CHAPTER TEN

Swift found the next few days even more enervating than Cordari had the earlier ones.

He realized that Manton was right and that Cordari must already be somewhere abroad; maybe even at his journey's end. Despite this, however, he fretted at the lack of news which accompanied each day. Moreover, it seemed to him that patience could be exercised too far and that Susannah should at least be brought in and questioned. But to every such suggestion Manton would shake his head and say: 'We've got to wait. If we don't hear anything within a week, then'll be time enough to think about pushing the old girl around. In any event she's almost certainly only a very small cog in the machine and probably knows very little of what's going on. And I'm not going to risk everything at this juncture for such a doubtful return.'

Instead he sent Swift out on that dullest but commonest duty in a young detective's life: to keep observation quietly and tenaciously—and unnoticed. Thus three mornings in succession Swift stood watch outside West End Court. And though he tried not to chafe at the inactivity, this became increasingly difficult as the hours passed.

In the course of them, he lost weary count of the number of

times each day Mr. Turnbull popped across the street between his office and the court. He got to learn Susannah's repertoire by heart, including the words of several of her songs. Also that Lord Droxford was driven to court every morning by his wife, an extremely chic-looking woman who kissed him warmly before letting him get out of the car. Ten minutes before this piece of routine, Mr. Astbury was always to be seen hurrying along the street from the direction of the Underground station, his folded paper tucked like a baton beneath his arm and his gaze fixed on the pavement a few yards ahead of his feet.

All this Swift noted, and more beside, though none of it of apparent significance. The third day, however, did bring a variation to Lord Droxford's routine when Swift saw him go up to Susannah before entering the building. He handed her some money and appeared to exchange a friendly word. After only a few moments he went inside, but for the next half-hour or so Swift's senses were doubly alert, as he watched in vain for some connecting incident.

The third morning of his vigil produced another matter of potential interest in the arrival at court of Joe Mendolia, accompanied by a couple of henchmen. He walked straight in and left again about twenty minutes later, looking cheerful and carefree. For several minutes he stood talking on the steps to Rex Turnbull, then, searching in his trouser pocket he extracted a coin, dropped it into Susannah's tin and walked off towards his car. As in the case of Lord Droxford earlier, however, none of these actions seemed to evoke any special response. A good many people gave Susannah money as they passed; nevertheless, for some reason she had been chosen as one of the instruments of contact with Cordari. . . .

Later, Swift learned that Mendolia's visit to court had been for the purpose of seeing how one of his rivals fared on a gambling charge.

It was during the court's luncheon adjournment each day that he used to go to a nearby post office and inquire at the post restante counter whether there was any mail for Giuseppe Skourasi. It had been arranged that he should pass as Rafaele's brother and that letters so addressed should be sent to him care of that particular post office.

Day after day the counter clerk would shake his head and say:

'I don't think so, but I'll just check. No, nothing.' But on the sixth day after Cordari's disappearance, he came back to the counter wearing a tolerant smile. 'You're in luck at last,' he said. 'There is one for you today.' And he handed Swift a letter.

Swift's heart leapt excitedly as he recognized Cordari's writing on the envelope and yet again when he saw the Algiers postmark and the stamps of that country.

He sped from the post office and hailed a passing cab. On the way to the Yard, he carefully slit the envelope with his pen-knife, after holding it up first to the light to make sure he could do so safely.

His fingers trembled as he pulled out the sheet of paper inside and unfolded it. It read:

Dear Brother,
    Am safe and well so don't worry about me, tho afraid it will be a big shock to you. Can't explain things yet but will send you money very soon. Please believe, brother, that I'm doing right thing, for God will surely grant us true happiness. Be patient, dear brother, for the sake of your innocent, Rafaele.

Manton slowly read through the letter a second time, and looked up at Swift, who was standing beside him.

'It's his handwriting all right.'

'No doubt about that, sir,' Swift replied. 'Would you like to interpret it?'

'You'd better do that—I'm more than intrigued by the bits about sending you money and the certainty that God is on our side.'

'Well, sir, the first sentence is no more than it says, namely that he's O.K. Then his reference to our having a big "shock" means that when he's able to tell us the whole story it's not going to be exactly as we'd imagined. We arranged he'd work in that particularly word if there were any surprise turns or anything of that sort.'

'But he's arrived in Algeria like the rest of them, so what surprise turns can there have been?'

'He may be referring to the route or the mode of travel, sir.'

'We didn't—in fact don't—know anything about either, so I can't quite see what can surprise us about them. However, go on.'

' "Can't explain things yet but will send money soon" means everything it says, sir, except that "money" stands for "further

41

report".' Manton nodded approvingly and Swift continued: 'The next sentence indicates that he's certain he's on to something and is confident, moreover, that the plan is going to work out successfully. And the final bit is a warning to us not to act at this end until we hear from him again, otherwise we may queer his pitch.'

'So it amounts to this: that everything's going according to plan; that he'll be getting in touch again soon and doesn't want us to do anything until he does. *And* that we're due for a few shocks when we do learn the truth.'

'That's about the strength of it, sir,' Swift agreed. 'Of course we couldn't evolve any rigid form of code as we didn't know how much he'd be able to write or in what circumstances he'd be doing so. We decided to restrict it to a few key words which could be worked into any old sort of letter.'

Manton had purposely left the detail of this to his young assistants, contenting himself merely with instructions that they must have some simple workable code at their disposal.

'The fact that he has used our code, sir,' Swift went on, 'shows that someone must have been looking over his shoulder when he wrote.'

'Or that he knew his letter would be subject to censorship. Not that there's anything particularly significant about that. Obviously, having got a client safely out of the country, they aren't going to risk detection through an indiscreet letter home.'

'How long do you reckon to give now, sir, before we hear again?'

'Three or four days at the outside.'

'And if we don't hear from him in that time, sir, what then?'

'We shall hear all right.'

But Manton was wrong. No further news came.

CHAPTER ELEVEN

Though Swift was not old enough to have any personal recollections of fighting in the Second World War, he imagined from all he'd heard that it wasn't so different from what was happening to him now. A period of boredom and frustration was about to give way to one of furious activity. And as is often the case where the spirit has fretted at inaction, it becomes perversely unsure, when faced with the reality of a sudden change, that the former state isn't, after all, the more desirable. So sinks the morale of armies; though to do Swift justice, it didn't last long with him.

Once over his initial shock at the prospect of action at last, he squared his shoulders and welcomed it, if not with enthusiasm at least with sturdy resolution.

For two hours ago he'd been suddenly told by Manton that he was to leave for Algeria the next morning. There had then followed two hours of hectic rush so that this was the first moment he'd had to 'phone Pamela.

As he held the receiver waiting for her to answer and wondering how many more 'brr-brrs' to allow before deciding she wasn't at home his heart began to sink. It was vital that he saw her before departing; and yet supposing he couldn't get hold of her, what then? A letter written from the airport? No, he'd got to find her, even it it meant combing the town all night. It was at this moment that he heard her voice on the line. It sounded cross.

'Hello.'

'Pamela, this is Kevin. I've got to see you. I'm going away.'

'When?'

'Tomorrow, early.'

'Will you be seeing Roy while you're gone?'

'Probably.'

There was a short silence. 'Come along this evening. I'll boil you an egg for supper.'

'That would be wonderful. You're not going out, then?'

'No.'

'But you're still in with Mendolia?'

'Of course. That's what you want, isn't it?'

Swift had noticed before that Pamela could assume a somewhat disconcerting tone and manner when she wished. This was one of the moments she chose to.

'Y-yes, of course it is,' he said feebly.

'Now, I'm going back to my bath. You've made me drip all over the hall and I'm shivering like a waif.'

So that was why she had sounded cross.

'Good Lord! Do you mean you've been standing there without anything on?'

'If you must know, I'm draped in two smallish towels.'

43

Swift gave a spluttering laugh. 'See you around eight o'clock, if that's all right. I've got a fair amount to attend to before I can get away.'

'Fine. Till then.'

By the time he did leave for Wimbledon he was all set for his next day's journey. Passport, tickets, money and a heap of instructions had been pressed upon him. Manton had taken him along to see the Assistant Commissioner (Crime), who as head of the C.I.D. of the Metropolitan Police had been kept in touch with the investigation since its inception.

The A.C. had wished him luck and trotted out some pieces of guide-book advice on travel abroad. But he appeared to be ill at ease during the interview. After Swift had left the room, he had turned to Manton and said doubtfully:

'It does rather seem we're sending him off into the blue. Particularly as he can't even speak French.'

'I know, sir, that you'd normally send an officer who could; certainly one more senior than Swift. Nevertheless, I'm sure it'd be a mistake to bring in someone fresh at this delicate juncture. After all, sir, Swift's been in it from the beginning, working closely with Cordari under my direction, and though he may be only a junior officer, he's a thoroughly resourceful one—I can vouchsafe that—and I reckon if anything can be found out, he's the best person to do it. And we've obviously got to do something, sir. It's five days since we had any news of Cordari and I'm worried about him.'

'With some reason. If anything has happened to him out there ... Well, I just hope to God that it hasn't. However, though I'm not particularly happy about sending Swift after him, I agree, on balance, that it's preferable to throwing the assignment at someone fresh. I can't help being influenced by the fact that we're not yet in a position to make any moves at an official level.'

'No, and we're not exactly dispatching him into the blue, sir. We've arranged for this man Roland to be at his disposal, and he sounds a useful type. With an English father, a French mother and an Arab wife, he should know his way around. And he's lived in the country for over twenty years. He did a good deal of under-cover work for us during the war, particularly around the time of the North African invasion.'

'What's he do for a living now?'

Manton opened a folder he had in his hand. 'Employment is given as "Various", sir.'

'I bet it has been, too. Anyway, I hope you're right about him. With those fellows it's usually a question of results according to payment.'

When Swift arrived at Pamela's flat that evening he found the table already laid for supper. Pamela was wearing a rust-coloured dress which, though not as obviously expensive as the green one of his previous visit, at least showed off as much of her figure. Swift followed her into the kitchen and watched while she put the finishing touches to their meal.

'Has anything happened to Roy?' she asked suddenly, without looking up from the tomato she was slicing.

There was an awkward silence.

'I hope not.'

'I'd far sooner you told me any bad news. You see, Doreen hasn't heard anything from him for over a week, and though he warned her he might not be able to write to her for some time, I was wondering . . .'

'Look, Pamela, I can't tell you what's happening, but—but— well, do you remember last time I was here, you made me promise to break any bad news to you first? That promise still stands. It's a fact Roy has temporarily disappeared, but that's all according to plan and it doesn't mean he's come to any harm.'

'But your sudden departure tomorrow wasn't part of the original plan, was it?' she asked, refusing to be thrown off the scent.

'It was always a possibility.'

'Well, as long as you keep your promise'—here she threw him a melting smile—'and I know you will, I'll try not to nag you any further on the subject.'

During the meal they talked of other things: of some of the jobs she had tried her hand at; of her views on Elvis Presley and on central heating, and of her passion for Siamese cats and dancing. In exchange, Kevin Swift related excerpts from his boyhood and told her with pride how his father had recently retired after thirty years' service as a policeman in one of the Northern county forces and taken up bee-keeping.

When the dishes were washed and they were together on the sofa, he said:

'Will you miss me when I'm away?'

She laughed, 'I expect so.'

'That's not very flattering.'

'I might have said "No", which would have been less so.'

'Have you ever thought about marriage?'

'What girl hasn't?'

'Well?'

'I take it this isn't a proposal?' she said in a tone of slight suspicion.

He shook his head. 'Not yet.'

'That's just as well. Anyway, you're in no condition to start proposing marriage.'

'What do you mean by that?'

'You're in one of those incurably sentimental moods that overcome males on the eve of their going off to battle and the like.'

'What's wrong with being sentimental?'

'Nothing at all, provided you don't mistake it for anything more than it is.'

'I won't argue,' he said, and edged a bit closer to her. Later she made no attempt to evade him when he leant forward and brought her head gently towards his. Their embrace was long and satisfying.

After some time he was aware that though she had responded with apparent enthusiasm to his kisses, she had remained throughout in complete control of her emotions.

As he leaned back against the cushions, she pulled the folded handkerchief out of his breast pocket and wiped his lips with it, rather like a mother cleaning her small boy's grubby face.

She looked at the red stains on the handkerchief and made a face.

'Mucky stuff lipstick is. If I'd thought I wouldn't have put on so much.'

Swift wanted to ask her if she was equally considerate towards Mendolia, but somehow funked the answer he might receive. He shrank from the idea that she had become his mistress or even allowed herself to be petted by him, and yet it was improbable that she could retain his interest otherwise. And yet again, surely . . . but speculation in the realms of female psychology would merely induce a headache. She was a strange girl; one didn't know what to think.

'It's time for you to go home,' she said with disconcerting suddenness. 'You've got to be up first thing in the morning and I'm due for an early night as well.' She noticed his reluctance to follow her example when she rose to her feet and put out a hand. 'Come.'

With a quick movement Swift pulled her down over him and hungrily sought her lips once more. She permitted him a short kiss, and then with a surprising turn of strength yanked him to his feet.

'Write to me, if you can,' she said in a tone as though she meant it. 'And that'll ensure I don't miss you too much.'

He followed her out into the hall.

'Don't let Joe Mendolia get up to any tricks while I'm away.'

She smiled in an abstracted fashion. 'By the time you get back I hope I have found out what you and Roy want to know. Joe's cagey, though, and it's slow work. I've dropped a number of hints about this smuggling racket, but he either laughs as though it's rather a good joke or else he doesn't respond at all. But leave it to me, Kevin; I'll get to the truth, even if I have to bust.'

'Where is he this evening?' Swift asked, feeling that he owed Mendolia something of a debt for Pamela's company.

She shook her head. 'I've no idea. That's what I've tried to explain to you: he doesn't tell me every detail of his life. He just says, "Shan't be able to see you tomorrow," or whatever it may be, and that's that.'

'He may even be out with another girl.'

She appeared to ponder this.

'It's possible, but I don't think so.' Shepherding him towards the front door she asked abruptly: 'Is it permitted to know where you're going? It would be much nicer if I could picture you in a definite place.'

'Algeria.'

'Algeria?' she said in a surprised tone. 'That's really rather a coincidence.'

'What is?'

'Well, Joe Mendolia mentioned it the other evening.' Swift's ears pricked with interest. 'Quite casually, I mean. It was when I was trying to pump him gently and I said something about West End Court and he made some remark about Lord Drox-ford being a real gent; and went on to mention that Lady Droxford was French and came from Algeria. He said her people were big landowners out there.'

Swift looked unusually thoughtful for a moment, then said:

'Yes, that does seem a bit of a coincidence.'

But was it anything more than that, he wondered, as he walked away from the house?

CHAPTER TWELVE

Apart from a school holiday spent on the Belgian coast and a few months' Army service in the British zone of Germany, Kevin Swift had never been out of England; this certainly being the first time he'd ventured forth alone. On the other occasions, he had always been as safely shepherded as any flock of prize sheep.

From the moment he arrived at London Airport, however, he felt that the whole place had been organized solely for the purpose of getting him on to the right 'plane. It was all delightfully simple, and was accomplished with well-practised charm.

There was but one fleeting moment of disenchantment, and that came when he discovered that the extremely attractive girl who had led his flight party through the multitudinous formalities was not going to accompany them on the journey.

She brought them across the few yards of tarmac to their waiting *Air France* 'plane and stood at the bottom of the steps, her duty done.

'Have a nice journey, sir,' she said to Swift, who'd been keeping as close to her as a shy child to its nannie.

'But aren't you coming too?' he asked.

She smiled. 'No such luck.'

Crestfallen, he made his way into the 'plane, selected a seat at the rear end, composing himself for the journey, went fast asleep.

He was awakened, when they were somewhere over central France, by the 'plane doing a feather-caught-in-a-draught act. He felt reassured when they'd crossed the mountains and were over the wide Rhone delta where the upper air was tranquil once more. Twenty minutes later they came down at Marseilles, where he was scheduled to change 'planes.

He soon found that London Airport is one thing and Marseilles quite another—at any rate to someone whose knowledge of French peters out after a dozen words. By the time he had

48

gathered (or thought he had, though he was never sure) that there wasn't a 'plane to Algiers for five hours he was exhausted, dishevelled and feeling distinctly homesick. He sat on a hard seat in the refreshment room and stared gloomily at advertisements round the walls which exhorted him to '*buvez*' a striking variety of beverages, alcoholic and otherwise. As each consisted of pictures of happy, smiling people setting him the example, he finally advanced on the counter and ordered by pointing at the nearest bottle. This proved to be Pernod, and though he found the taste of it awful the effect was splendid.

Thereafter, from time to time, he took short turns outside where the sun was blazing down on the flat, brown landscape, and there was absolutely nothing of social interest to beguile either eye or ear. It might have been any of several thousand airports in the hotter corners of the world.

Whenever a 'plane landed and drew up before the small airport building, he would search frantically for a sympathetic face whose owner might be able to enlighten him further about his prospects of getting to Algiers. He had long since given up trying to get anything out of the offhand young man who purported to be the airline's official representative on duty and whose few words of English were so grudgingly spoken as to produce an immediate impasse in any efforts at communication.

What surprised Swift, as he now turned away from a helpful man in a blue beret and khaki shorts who'd reassured him that the presently loading 'plane was not his, was the manner in which the crowds gathered and dispersed. One moment he would seem to have the whole aerodrome to himself. The next, it would be a mass of jostling people, far more in number than ever got on or off any 'plane in sight.

It was a puzzle that remained unsolved. All he knew was that at six o'clock he was one of a throng converging on a squat double-décker 'plane, which was, he prayed, bound for Algiers.

During the journey across the Mediterranean he lay back in his seat with a splitting headache and mounting apprehension, for both of which the Pernod was to some extent responsible. The 'plane was noisy and packed with whole French families who were returning to their North African homes after visiting relatives in France. Many of them looked worried, as well they might in view of the troubled state of their country—the country that was theirs by birth or adoption. Once they were back, things wouldn't seem quite so bad, but reading about the massacres, assassinations and outrages while they'd been away had been unnerving.

Swift opened his eyes and looked out. There was a string of lights below, which could only mean that the shores of North Africa had been reached at last. Then the 'plane circled over Algiers itself and came in to land at Maison Blanche Airport.

Ten minutes later, as though by the waving of a wand, Swift's morale took a soaring rise when a friendly figure suddenly stepped out of the waiting crowd and claimed him.

'Mr. Swift? I'm Roland. Had a good trip? Expect you're glad it's over. Tiring business, flying. Come on, we'll soon have you through this lot. Not sticky like the British Customs, provided you're not suspected of gun-running for the "fellagahs".'

Throughout the twenty-minute run into Algiers Mr. Roland kept up an easy flow of non-stop comment on a wide variety of innocuous topics. Swift lay back in his seat and listened with a weary but contented spirit. The object of his visit was never mentioned. Work, presumably, could await the morning.

He awoke the next day just before six. The sun was well up and he felt more than ready to face life once more. He clambered out of bed and went through the male routine of yawning, stretching and having a luxurious scratch before crossing the room to the window and peering out.

Beyond knowing that he was at the Pension Bayonne and that it stood back from the street in its own garden, he had no idea what to expect. Mr. Roland had given him the first piece of information and the other he had noted when they drove up the previous evening.

The view that now met his eyes was indeed superb, being enhanced by the fresh, clear, morning air. Half left was a distant sweep of shimmering blue sea. Immediately in front of the *pension,* the ground fell away in terraced gardens to what appeared to be a business sector, and off to the right in the rim of an encircling hill were a number of handsome new apartment houses. All the buildings that met his gaze shone white in the morning sunlight.

It was a scene of beauty and serenity with which it was impossible to associate any of the horrors of terrorism. And yet behind some of the very walls he now gazed at, deeds of inhuman cruelty were probably being planned. As he shaved in cold water at the small wash-basin by the window, his thoughts turned to Cordari and to where he might be at this moment. Was he still in Algeria—perhaps even in Algiers itself; or had he by now moved on another square in the strange game?

When he was dressed, Swift went downstairs and out into the garden, which was planted with orange and lemon trees and had iron tables and chairs dotted around in such shade as existed. Further reconnaissance revealed that life was just beginning to stir in the kitchen.

He pulled one of the chairs into the sun, lit his pipe and sat down to ponder while waiting for his breakfast. This was brought to him in due course by an old Arab (in fact a Kabyle from the mountain region of Algeria which bears the same name), who had a worn appearance but with it a delightful expression of twinkling detachment which seemed to suggest an equal acceptance of life's buffets and favours. He put a tray of crusty bread, butter and coffee before Swift, chattering all the while in curious French. Swift grinned back and the old man went away chuckling, after an elaborate mime in which he pointed vigorously down his throat and patted his stomach.

Swift was just finishing the meal when Mr. Roland arrived.

'Thought I'd probably find you up and about. Expect you'd like to get down to business. Gather you're trying to trace someone out here. Is that right?'

'Yes.'

'Where do you want to start?'

In suitably guarded terms, Swift told him of the letters which had been received with the Algiers' postmark and of his wish to find out anything he could about their origin.

'Have you got any of the envelopes with you?'

'Three, including the one received last week.' Swift took them from his pocket and passed them over. Mr. Roland studied each with care, as Swift for the first time took the opportunity of examining Mr. Roland. He was a short, thick-set man with a pronounced paunch. His face was leathery and his hair grey-cropped, and he wore a grubby shirt, open at the neck, a creased linen jacket, a pair of ridiculously short khaki drill trousers, no socks and some ancient plimsolls.

'I might be able to help you,' he said, putting the envelopes down on the table. 'Incidentally, think I'll join you for breakfast.' He gave a shout, and when the old servant appeared spoke to him rapidly in a tongue Swift didn't reconize but presumed to be Arabic. 'Yes, I think I might be able to help you,' he went

51

on, watching Swift carefully and pouring himself out some coffee.

'I am, of course, prepared to recompense you for your services,' Swift replied, with an Englishman's stilted diffidence at having to mention to a stranger anything as sordid as money.

Mr. Roland appeared to weigh the situation as he chewed on a well-buttered crust.

'The car and other expenses last night came to over two thousand francs,' he said.

Swift was about to expostulate that he understood a substantial advance had already been sent to cover such items, but finally decided it was probably worth the taxpayers' money—within reason—to keep Mr. Roland sweet. He fished a five-thousand-france note out of his pocket and handed it over.

'Shall we go?' Mr. Roland asked, with the promptness of a slot machine responding to the inserted coin.

'Were to?'

'I have a friend in the head post office down town who may be able to give us a lead.'

As they got up and walked towards the gate, the old Arab servant came running after them. He and Mr. Roland spoke together for a moment and then he turned back to the house, chuckling merrily to himself. Swift felt pretty sure that instructions had been given for Mr. Roland's breakfast and all future entertainment to be chalked up to him.

On the way down town, Mr. Roland was a gay and informative companion, indicating places of interest that they passed.

'It's a beautiful city, isn't it?' he said proudly at one point. 'A wonderful natural site for North and South to meet and merge.'

It was indeed beautiful, Swift thought, as he gazed fascinated at the diversity of the scene. There was definitely something mysterious, too, as the travel books always tritely emphasized, about the heavily veiled women whose eyes peered furtively from behind their cover. Eyes that seemed always to be taking in, but to be careful to give nothing away. On the other hand the male Arab—at any rate all those over about sixteen—looked to Swift undisguisedly sly and sinister.

'Of course there's some pretty mixed blood here,' Mr. Roland said. 'In fact I'm responsible for some of it myself. You've probably been told my wife's Arab.' Before Swift could comment, he went on: 'This area here on our left is the Casbah—the original part of Algiers. It covers the whole of that hill.'

Swift looked up a narrow street where people thronged and houses were clustered like fungi. It was another world from the fine wide boulevard they were walking along and put him in mind of an extremely active ant-heap.

'Is it safe to go walking in there alone?' he asked.

'For me, yes. For you, probably; though it mightn't be a very comfortable experience. So much depends on their mood of the moment. They could be all quiet now, and in a state of dangerous ferment before we reach the end of this street. Trouble can blow up as quickly as that. On the whole, you can say they're rather like bees. Always buzzing, but unlikely to sting you unless you poke a stick among them.'

'You don't live in the Casbah?'

'Not now. I have done, mind you. Did until just before the war, in fact.'

'What's that great building that looks like a wedding cake?' Swift asked suddenly.

'That's where we're going. It's the post office.'

They went round to a side entrance and Mr. Roland told Swift to wait just inside the door while he went to see if his friend was available. He returned a few minutes later accompanied by a tall young man with a tiny head and toothbrush moustache.

'This is Monsieur Gazaux. He thinks he may be able to help you. We'll go across to the café opposite and he'll come to us there when he can get away.'

It wasn't long before M. Gazaux joined them and accepted the drink which Mr. Roland ordered at Swift's expense. He solemnly examined the three envelopes that were handed to him.

'All posted at the main office here,' he said, without apparent interest. 'Let me keep them and meet you back here at twelve. I may be able to tell you more then.' With this, he got up and left them.

Mr. Roland suggested that in the meantime he should take Swift on a sightseeing tour of the city. Together they set off and in due course wandered through a section of the Casbah. As they threaded their way along the narrow, densely filled streets, Swift silently acknowledged that he would not have cared to be there alone, nor, for that matter, with a companion less self-assured than Mr. Roland. It was easy to imagine it as a district into which innocents strayed and vanished for ever.

By the time they got back to the café it was five minutes to twelve and Swift's tongue was hanging out.

M. Gazaux arrived on the minute, this time carrying a brief-case and wearing a pair of dark glasses. He sat down, flicked his fingers at a waiter and extracted the three envelopes from the briefcase. He said:

'It would have been easier if any of these letters had been posted in other than a big town, you understand, for then they'd have borne the postmark of some place where it wouldn't be so difficult to find out their origin.' He addressed himself in French direct to Mr. Roland, who translated, and while this was going on M. Gazaux stared about him in a coldly reproving way. 'However, it is possible I have discovered something which may assist your friend. One of the counter clerks has an English friend who comes in about once a month and always attends at his desk. I say "friend", but he does not know his name. It is the same way that one refers to the postman or the bus driver as a "friend". One talks to him and knows about his wife's pains, his children's problems; everything—except his name.' Swift nodded understandingly, and M. Gazaux went on: 'The Englishman has bought stamps from this clerk, you under-stand, and the clerk has observed him sticking the stamps on to letters destined for England.' M. Gazaux paused and wrinkled his nose in an expression which seemed to disclaim all personal responsibility for what he was saying. 'This clerk has had occa-sion to notice that the letters have been in different hand-writings—in different English handwritings, he says. He cannot, you understand, positively recognize *these* three letters as being any of those actually stamped in his presence by the English-man. But . . .' The sentence was completed by a gallic shrug of the shoulders and an expressive projection of M. Gazaux's lower lip.

'Does the clerk know where this Englishman lives?' Swift asked.

'*Mais oui,*' M. Gazaux replied without waiting for Mr. Roland to translate. 'He lives near Ourasa.'

'That's a small town on the coast about forty miles west of here,' Mr. Roland explained.

'He is a clerk on a farm there,' M. Gazaux went on. 'My colleague doesn't know the name of this farm, you understand, but the Englishman did once mention to him in conversation something about the owner being connected with a judge's wife in England.'

Swift sat up with a start, his eyes brightly alert. He had been wondering how much time and effort he ought to spend in pursuit of the shadowy Englishman. Now, however, all doubt was cast aside. He must find him at all costs.

To Swift's annoyance, Mr. Roland said the expedition to Ourasa couldn't be organized till the next day. It would take time, he said, to arrange a car. Morever, it was going to require at least a full day to execute such an uncertain quest.

'Well, if we set off this afternoon, we can spend the night there and be on the spot for an early start tomorrow,' Swift argued.

'Spend the night where?' Mr. Roland asked mildly.

'In an hotel at Ourasa.'

'Yes, that was that I thought you had in mind. But I'm afraid you won't find an hotel there—at least not one you'd care to stay in. Be patient, my friend, you're not going to lose anything in half a day. And I'm sure, anyway, you can spend a profitable afternoon writing a report of events so far. Your superiors in London will be waiting to hear from you. Cheer up, we have made a good start.'

With a sigh, Swift gave up; though honours, he felt, were evenly divided in the end when he firmly refused Mr. Roland's solicitation of an advance of cash, required, so he said, to ensure the success of the next day's arrangements.

He spent the afternoon back at the hotel, composing a report for Manton and writing a long letter to Pamela.

The following morning he was again up early, but was then kept hanging about at the front gate for half an hour waiting for the car to come.

When finally it did arrive, there was no Mr. Roland—only the driver, a smooth-faced, curly headed young Arab with a wide mouth and gleaming white teeth.

'Mr. Roland?' Swift asked, giving the name his best French accent.

'Not coming,' the youth said in surprisingly good English. 'I take you.'

'You know where we're going?'

'To Ourasa, to find the Englishman.'

Doubtless he'd get on just as well without Mr. Roland, Swift reflected. Maybe he'd even do better without him, provided the driver helped out over the language problem.

55

'You can speak French, I suppose?'

'And Spanish and Arabic,' the youth replied with a grin.

'What's your name?'

'Ahmed.'

'O.K., Ahmed, let's be off,' he said, getting in beside him and closing the door. The effect was that of digging a pair of spurs into a lively young colt. The car (though, in fact, anything but young) leapt from the kerb with Ahmed leaning forward over the wheel in an attitude of eager intensity.

They drove westwards out of the city and along the coast road, passing every few miles through small, straggling towns where Arabs lounged in doorways and gazed impassively at their reckless progress. From time to time they had pleasing views of sparkling blue sea on their right. On the opposite side of the road the ground rose gently for about a mile. This slope was sometimes wooded, sometimes terraced with vines and citrus trees. Beyond it, the terrain fell away out of sight to the broad fertile plain which in turn stretched back to the foothills of the Atlas Mountains some fifteen to twenty miles inland.

It was shortly before nine o'clock when Ahmed halted the car in the main street of a small town, which had an air of greater prosperity than most of the others they had passed through.

'Is this Ourasa?' Swift asked. Ahmed nodded. Swift looked out and saw they were halted outside a newly white-washed building labelled in large black letters: '*Bureau de Poste*'. 'Do we ask here?'

'Yes; come.' Ahmed got out and headed straight towards the entrance.

'Hey, wait a minute. I've got to decide, first, exactly what we're going to ask.'

'Come,' Ahmed said, with a beckoning gesture of his head and disappeared inside the building.

Swift ran in after him. Inside, the place was deserted and the air smelt cool and musty, as though it had been bottled for some thousand years and just released. A large, burly man suddenly came into view behind the grille and stared at them suspiciously. Ahmed leant easily against the counter and broke into a torrent of French. As he spoke, the official, who, despite the atmosphere, was glistening at every pore, cast Swift appraising glances. When Ahmed finished, he said:

'*Vous êtes anglais?*' Swift nodded. '*Et vous cherchez* Monsieur Heath?'

Swift looked appealingly at Ahmed.

'He asks if you search for Mr. Heath?'

'Mr. Heath? Is that the name of the Englishman who works on a farm near here?' Events had moved quickly, and Swift felt in danger of losing control of them. 'Have you explained everything to him, then? I mean, are you sure Mr. Heath is the man we're after?'

Ahmed turned back to the man and had a further conversation with him.

'He says Mr. Heath is the only Englishman he knows in this area. He works for Monsieur de Varin.'

'Do you think this gentleman would tell us more about Mr. Heath if we were to ask him?' Swift said.

'No. He already becomes a little suspicious. I told him you were from the British Consulate in Algiers, but now I think he does not know whether to believe it.'

And with some reason, thought Swift. Though he knew nothing of the habits of consular officials, he imagined they didn't drive around on business in dilapidated Citroëns, wearing sports jackets and no ties. Anyway, if Mr. Heath was the only Englishman in the district, Mr. Heath was going to receive a visit.

'Do you know where Mr. de Varin's farm is?' Swift asked. Ahmed nodded and turned to leave the post office. Swift followed him after an attempt to allay their informant's suspicions with a disarming smile.

Outside, a throng of Arabs of all ages had gathered. They stared at Swift with interest while Ahmed apparently explained who he was. One or two of the older ones, who, Swift thought, looked thoroughly villainous, never took their eyes off him.

'Come on, Ahmed, let's be on our way,' he said impatiently. As he pushed his way to the car a string of clamorous urchins wheeled about him. 'Here you are, then, you little pests,' he said, finally counting out the smallest coins in his pocket. 'Do you know where to go?' he asked, when at last they drove off.

'Two kilometres from here we find Monsieur de Varin's farm.'

The entrance to it was a dirt track which led from the road towards a group of barn-like buildings a quarter of a mile away. Ahmed drove up and stopped the car outside one of these and shouted through the window at a row of Arab workers who were sitting propped against the wall. One of them called back and there then ensued what sounded to Swift a thoroughly unproductive duologue.

'He's not here,' Ahmed said over his shoulder, and immediately plunged back into his conversation with a renewed fervour.

Swift realized there was nothing he could do but await the outcome, for it had recently been borne in upon him that, apart from the language barrier, there was another, equally insurmountable; namely the difference in outlook, character and reaction between himself and the indigenous population. A whole new approach had to be learnt before one could begin to make headway in the realm of co-operative effort. It was much more than just learning a language.

'He's at the fig farm,' Ahmed said, shouting a final word at the men and turning the car round. 'This is where they make the wine,' he went on before Swift could reply, indicating the buildings. Indeed it was possible to glimpse huge vats with catwalks and great pipes snaking around them.

'What fig farm?' Swift asked.

'Monsieur de Varin's fig farm. It is another five kilometres down the road.'

They regained the road and turned left.

'Monsieur de Varin's home,' Ahmed said a few minutes later, pointing at a large white house with bright green shutters standing on a small eminence which jutted out into the sea. Steps led down to a private beach, and a yacht was anchored close to the shore. 'Very rich man, with many farms.'

As they went past the entrance, Swift saw a beautifully laid out garden with a tennis court and beside it a swimming pool. It was certain there was no lack of money here. They drove on. Ahmed scanning the road ahead. With a sudden grunt of satisfaction, he swung the car sharply up a steep narrow track which led to a sort of outsize potting-shed. An Arab in a large straw hat appeared round one corner.

Once more there was a lengthy interlocution through the car window. While it was going on, Swift saw a man coming down the track towards them. He was wearing an old topee, with khaki shirt and shorts. He spoke to the Arab, who nodded in the direction of the car.

'Are you inquiring for me?' he asked in French. Swift got out and came round to where the man was standing.

'Mr. Heath?' he asked.

'Yes.' Then, after a slight pause: 'You sound English.'

'I am. My name's Swift. I wonder if I might have a word with you alone, Mr. Heath?'

There was something weary, even resigned, about Mr. Heath's finely drawn features as he pondered the request.

'We can go and talk under that tree if you wish,' he said nodding in the direction of a large acacia. 'There's nowhere else much.'

'That'll do.' Swift turned towards the car, in which Ahmed still sat. 'You wait here for me.'

As he and Heath walked towards the tree, Swift decided on his line of approach. He would be direct and tackle the man without any ceremony.

'Did you by any chance post these?' he asked, producing the three envelopes with a conjurer's sleight of hand. Heath gazed at them for what seemed an interminable time, then lifted his head and looked out across the sea with an expression of pensive melancholy. His face seemed suddenly to have aged several years and he looked tired and ill.

'What if I did?' he said with apparent effort. 'And, anyway, who are you?'

'I'm trying to trace the men who wrote these letters.'

'Then I can't help you.'

'But you posted them,' Swift said. Without turning his head, Heath gave the envelopes a further sidelong look and Swift went on in a pressing tone: 'And one of them within the last week.' Like someone leading the ace of trumps, he now plucked the one in Cordari's writing and held it up challengingly. 'You posted them all at the main post office in Algiers. The counter clerk there remembers you.' For this was near enough the truth.

'Is that how you traced me?'

Swift nodded, and silence ensued. As they stood there in the shadow of the acacia he began to feel encompassed by a strange air of unreality. The car was temporarily hidden from view and the broad sweeping landscape was uncannily still. He almost had the sensation, standing there and gazing out over the sea, that they were the last two mortals left on the African continent. He suddenly felt that all urgency had drained away, that he and Heath were in a timeless vacuum where questions and answers were no more than the mechanical moves in a sleepwalker's dream. At last Heath spoke.

59

'I tell you I can't help you. I don't know where they are,' he said.

'They?' said Swift sharply.

'The men who wrote these letters,' he repeated dully, 'I don't know where they are.'

'You mean they've left? They're no longer in the country?'

'Left?' said Heath stupidly. 'No, they haven't left. But they aren't here either.' He looked obliquely at Swift and for the first time showed some agitation. 'They've never been here at all.'

While Swift was still mentally chasing the implications of this, Heath continued : 'Are you something to do with the police?'

'Yes.' There seemed to be no point in denying it.

'I see. And you're looking for the men who wrote those letters. And since they were posted in Algiers, you naturally assumed the men had themselves come here.' Though this was more in the nature of thinking aloud than anything else, Swift waited for him to finish. As he watched him, it passed through Swift's mind that he certainly didn't have the air of being a high-up in any gang's organization. At best, he was likely to be only an unimportant and dispensable cog.

'These men have disappeared out of England, Mr. Heath. What do you know about it?'

'Nothing, nothing, I tell you. I don't know where they are.'

'Then explain how you came to post the letters. Incidentally, am I right in supposing you've posted others apart from these three?'

'Yes, about six altogether.'

'Now let's have the whole story.'

Looking utterly submissive Heath said:

'I received the letters from England in sealed envelopes which were already addressed, and all I had to do was stamp and post them.'

'Who sent them to you?'

'I don't know.'

'That's ridiculous——'

'But it's the truth. About six or seven months ago, I got an anonymous letter saying I could earn myself some easy money by posting back to England letters which would be sent to me from time to time. There was no address and no name on the letter, but, soon after I got another. In the envelope were five one-pound notes and one of these letters for posting. Nothing else. So I stamped it and posted it. And that's all I've done in every case.' He paused and wiped the perspiration from his face. 'I promise you I never knew who wrote the letters. Why, the first time I even knew they were by persons who've left England was when you told me just now.'

'If that's so,' Swift said thoughtfully, 'it must have been all part of a ruse to throw us right off scent; to make us believe they'd come to Algeria when in fact they were smuggled to somewhere quite different.' With a new note of suspicion in his voice, he added: 'How did this anonymous person in England come to pick you for this job?'

Heath shook his head in weary hopelessness. 'I've no idea.'

'But you must have. How long have you lived here?'

'Just over two years.'

'Did you come from England?'

'Yes.'

'What were you there? Where did you live?' He raised his eyes to Heath's. 'In fact, who are you?'

'I lived in London. I used to be an usher at one of the courts.'

'Which?' Swift asked, with a catch in his tone.

'At West End. Lord Droxford's court.'

CHAPTER THIRTEEN

If one piece of the puzzle had now fallen into place, it triggered off in Swift's brain a whole series of fresh questions.

'How do you come to be living in Algeria and to have a job on this farm? It belongs to a Monsieur de Varin, doesn't it? And incidentally what exactly *do* you do?'

'I'm one of the clerks. I had to come to a warm climate on account of my health.'

'Yes, yes, but why Algeria? It's French. Why didn't you go to Malta or Gibraltar?'

Heath sighed heavily and fiddled with the array of pens and pencils which protruded from his breast pocket.

'I suppose it's got to come out,' he said with bitter despair. 'My employer, Monsieur de Varin, is Lord Droxford's brother-in-law. Lady Droxford was a de Varin before her marriage. She

61

was born in that house you passed down the road. When I left West End Court, Lord Droxford was good enough to arrange for me to come here. He'd always been extremely kind to me and he was never more so than when I had to retire.'

Something made Swift look at him again. Sick man he might be, but he was certainly not any older than the mid-forties. And he'd already been out here two years.

'Why did you have to retire?' he asked quietly. 'It wasn't only because of ill heath, was it?'

Though this had been something of a shot in the dark, Heath's crucified expression at once gave him away.

'I ran into a spot of trouble as well,' he said stiffly.

Feeling suddenly sorry for the man, Swift said coaxingly:

'It couldn't have been very bad trouble if Lord Droxford was ready to help you come out here.'

'I was weak and became an easy prey to temptation,' Heath went on, without appearing to hear. 'I always have been weak-willed. I know that. It's to do with my health. A sick body breeds a sick spirit. But I won't embarrass you with self-pity. What happened was, I gave someone some information I shouldn't have. It all seemed quite harmless at the time. I was offered ten pounds to find out, if I could, what evidence a police officer was going to give in a certain case. As you probably know, officers are in and out of court all the time and I knew the officer in question pretty well, and—well, to cut an unhappy story short, I was badly let down and was forced to resign.'

'Who was the person paying you for this information?'

'That was the tricky part. It was a defendant. A man named Mendolia.' He observed Swift's change of expression. 'I gather you've heard of him.'

'I have indeed.'

'I'm not surprised. He made himself pretty well known to the police.'

'Do you think it's possible that he's the person who's been sending you these letters for posting? He could be, I suppose?'

Heath's shoulders sagged in a gesture of further hopelessness.

'I've no idea who it is. It might be Mendolia, it might be any one of dozens of wicked-minded people who knew about my past and are determined I shan't be allowed to forget it, either.'

His tone was so odiously self-pitying that it was all Swift could do to refrain from pointing out that it would probably be more apt to describe such a person as a practical soul who obviously knew Heath's price. Instead he asked:

'Did many people know the truth about your resignation?'

'It never got into the Press, if that's what you mean. But everyone at West End Court knew, and also the people who put me in the cart like Mendolia and his lot.'

'Who was Mendolia's lawyer in the case?'

'Mr. Turnbull. He has offices opposite the court. But you needn't think he's mixed up in anything shady. He's a real gentleman, like Lord Droxford, however crooked some of his clients may be. He always treated me royally all the time I was at West End.'

'And what about the chief clerk?'

'Mr. Astbury's all right. Nothing wrong with him, once you got to know his little ways. Look, don't think I'm trying to tell you your job, but why should anyone connected with the court want me to do this?'

'Maybe it isn't anyone there,' Swift agreed, 'but after all, you've said yourself that not many people outside knew of the real reason for your retirement.'

'It's not fair putting it like that: saying the *real* reason, as though my health had nothing to do with it. I was a very sick man at the time. I still am a sick man.' His voice rose with each sentence and a tiny speck of froth appeared at the corner of his mouth as he continued to work himself up. Suddenly he thrust his head at Swift like an angry goose. 'Tell me, do I look a fit man? Do I look robust and brimming with good health?'

'No, you don't,' Swift answered, with embarrassment.

'Well, then, all this talk of *real* reason just isn't fair, is it?'

Swift decided he'd better switch to a less controversial subject. 'Used an old Negress to play the squeeze-box outside the court when you worked there?'

'Susannah, you mean? What's she got to do with this?'

'Probably nothing, but I just wanted to know.'

'Everyone knew Susannah,' Heath said in a reminiscent tone. 'She could recognize us all by our footsteps, long before we got to court. That is, the regulars. Is she still going strong?'

Swift nodded. 'She seems to be one of Nature's indestructibles.'

'She'll be interested to know you've seen me,' Heath said with odd complacency.

Swift felt he'd like to probe further the reasons for Heath having so readily accepted the role of letter-poster, but shrank from the self-pity and feeble self-justification this would undoubtedly evoke. And after all, he reflected, there probably was no more to know about that particular subject. Heath, it appeared, had always had his price, and now with all the added difficulties of life in exile he wasn't likely to turn away five pounds a time for posting a letter. To post or not to post, that had apparently been the clear-cut issue, without any 'ifs' or 'buts'. No, perhaps there wasn't any need to pursue the matter further. Provided Heath had been telling the truth (and Swift personally believed that he had), then his motives were sufficiently clear.

Swift took a deep breath and let his gaze roam over the peaceful scene. Two small boats had now appeared off shore. They were very still, and by screwing up his eyes he was able to see that each held a fisherman.

Noticing the direction of his look, Heath said:

'A couple of Arabs fishing for their supper.' Then he, too, slowly surveyed the whole tranquil scene. 'It's a very beautiful and unspoilt coastline, isn't it?'

'It certainly is. And after reading all that about terrorism out here, it's difficult to believe it's the same land.'

'Eastern Algeria has been the worst for that. This area has been relatively quiet. There've been outrages on some of the farms round here, mind you. Why, Monsieur de Varin himself had a case of arson on his biggest farm back in the plain.' He waved a hand in the direction of the hill-crest behind them. 'No one was killed, but a lot of damage was done, and worse still—and this, of course, was the whole object of it—it unsettled the Arab workers. And he employs over a thousand of them all told.'

Swift made some suitable comment, but all the while his brain was hard at work. What else should he try to find out before taking his leave and driving back to Algiers? He tried to think of all the questions Manton would expect him to ask, for it would be humiliating to arrive home and be met with pained surprise at what was considered a marked superficiality about his inquiries. But he could think of nothing.

'What's that building there?' he asked, pointing at the potting-shed, to give himself a bit more time to think.

An almost sly look came into Heath's eyes, only to vanish again immediately.

'Come along and I'll show you.'

They stepped out of the shadow of the acacia and walked

slowly down the track. As they appeared round the end of the building, two Arabs stepped forward. Heath said something to them in a tongue which Swift didn't recognize. Then opening a small door, he motioned Swift to follow him in. The heat inside was such that Swift found himself taking panic gulps of breath which only served, however, to make him feel worse. The noise too was ferocious.

'This is a fig-drier,' Heath shouted above the din. He pointed at a thermometer on the wall. 'It's a very dicy operation. They have to be in here for just the right length of time and at just the right temperature. Otherwise the whole crop can be ruined.'

Swift nodded abstractedly and moved towards the door.

'Here, come round the other side and I'll show you how it works.'

Reluctantly he followed Heath round and stood in desiccated discomfort while he explained the vagaries of fig-drying.

When at last they emerged, Swift felt he'd never been so near to becoming a dried fig himself. Heath watched him recover with apparent amusement.

'If I'd shut the door and left you in there, that might have been the last anyone would've heard of you,' he said, giving Swift a darting glance as he spoke. 'You wouldn't have lasted long in that heat, you know.'

This Swift could readily believe, but for a moment or two he was too intent on recovering to offer any comment of his own.

'I gather you're telling me how easily you could have murdered me,' he remarked, as they moved away.

Heath smiled wanly. 'I've often thought what a good way it would be of killing someone.'

'A crematorium oven would be even better.' He started to walk towards the car, where Ahmed lay sleeping in the back seat. Heath came slowly after him.

'Are you returning to Algiers now?'

'Yes. There doesn't seem to be anything further to be learnt out here.'

'Do you know, you're the first Englishman I've talked to in eight months. One doesn't meet many in this country. It probably sounds odd my saying this to you, in the circumstances, but I've enjoyed our talk.'

'No, I think I can understand that.'

'Even though you have dragged up my past and reminded me of much that was best forgotten. I feel I ought to offer you hospitality, but I live on one of the other farms and can't leave here yet.'

'Are you married?'

'My wife died soon after we arrived here,' he said quietly. 'I hope you accept all I've told you as being true and will try to keep my name out of your further inquiries.'

For once self-pity gave way to simple dignity, and Swift responded in kind. He was about to get into the car when Heath fumbled in his hip pocket and brought out a pound note.

'If you're returning to England soon, perhaps you'd do me a favour and change this. I can only do it at one of the banks in Algiers, and as I'm not very often in the city it would be a great help to me.'

There was no reason why Swift shouldn't agree to the transaction; yet he suddenly became oddly suspicious of it. 'Is it one you received from England?' he said.

'Yes it came with the last but one letter I was sent to post.'

'But if you had to go into Algiers to post the letter why couldn't you have changed the money then?'

'The banks were closed that day. And since then I've always forgotten to take it with me.'

It was ridiculous to make such a fuss about a trivial currency deal, but somehow the glibness of Heath's reply put him further on his mettle.

'But if that's so, why are you asking me to change only one pound?' Even as he spoke he felt resentful at being forced into such pettiness. What did it matter to him why the man wanted to change only one? But Heath now gave him a sickly smile and said:

'I'm afraid I haven't quite told you the truth. I changed four of the notes sent me when I posted the letter, but this one they wouldn't accept.' He opened it out. 'You can see it's badly torn and not very well stuck together again. But you won't have any trouble about getting rid of it at home.'

'O.K.,' Swift said, taking it from him and handing over the equivalent amount in francs. Though the tenacity of his questions had demonstrated Heath's capacity for skipping from one stupid lie to another, he had no sense of triumph in having finally flushed out the truth.

He bade Heath an uneasy farewell and got into the car. As they drove off, leaving the ex-usher forlornly staring after them, Swift tucked the pound note away in an inner pocket.

CHAPTER FOURTEEN

Swift observed little of the ride back to Algiers, his mind revolving ceaselessly round what he'd recently learnt from Heath, a man whose whole life and appearance so clearly spelt failure.

Above all, he was now more than ever worried about his friend, Roy Cordari. Of course, it was possible there'd been news of him during the last two or three days, but somehow Swift couldn't believe so. The knowledge that one of the letters in his pocket—a letter in Cordari's own hand and written so short a time ago—had been posted in this distant continent by someone who'd never even heard the names Cordari or Skourasi filled him with deep forboding. What the import of it all was he had no idea, but clearly it could be nothing good. Girls who vanish in similar circumstances became merchandise in the white-slave market and were popularly supposed to end up in South American brothels. But men? For what wicked purpose could men be smuggled out of England?

With the onset of anxiety came a sense of loneliness and a great yearning to be back home again. As soon as Ahmed had dropped him back at the Pension Bayonne and had departed (after submitting an impudent account for his services, which Swift, however, had been in no mood to quibble about) he booked a call to Manton in London.

When this came through and he had explained everything that had happened and answered a number of questions, he was relieved to hear Manton say:

'Well, there doesn't seem to be any point in your remaining out there. You'd better get a 'plane back as soon as you can. Tomorrow, if possible. Meanwhile, I'll report to the A.C.' There followed a pause. 'This needs a lot of thinking about. At the moment, I don't like the look of things at all.'

And still less did Swift, now Manton had told him that nothing further had been heard from Cordari.

It was only when he replaced the receiver and returned to his bedroom that he realized he needed Mr. Roland's services in arranging his passage home. He looked at his watch. It showed half past six. He went downstairs again and sought out Madame Bartisolles, who ran the establishment. He found her in the small room which served as a private office.

67

'Mr. Roland?' he asked with a wealth of accompanying gesture.

'*Oui, il est très gentil, n'est-ce pas?*' she said genially.

Swift smiled resignedly and tried again.

'Mr. Roland? *Où?*' he said.

'*Où est M. Roland? Vous Voulez le retrouver?*'

Uncertain whether he was on the right track, Swift now jabbed at his breast with a forefinger. 'Me,' he said. Then pointing vigorously out of the window with the same finger, he added: 'Mr. Roland.'

'*Oui, oui, je comprends, monsieur.*' She searched among the papers on her desk, found what she wanted and wrote an address down on the back of an old envelope. '*Venez, monsieur,*' she said, leading the way out of the house. On the pavement, she gave him a series of complicated instructions and then gently propelled him so that he at least started off in the right direction.

At length, after half an hour's exhausting search, he arrived at the address which he'd been given. It was in a mixed quarter of the city where Europeans and Arabs lived side by side. The street was alive with scrambling children and old people sitting in their doorways.

A small boy with huge brown eyes was unconcernedly urinating against the front of the house Swift sought. He waited for the boy to finish.

'Mr. Roland?' he asked, pointing at the house. For answer, the lad darted inside and a moment later Mr. Roland appeared.

'Why, hello, Mr. Swift. I was coming round to see you later this evening.'

'I've got to get a 'plane back to England as soon as possible. Tomorrow early if I can.'

'Such a short stay. What a shame. We'd better see what we can do. I'll come down town with you.' He turned uncertainly towards the interior of the house and then back to Swift. 'Do you mind coming in for a few moments while I get ready? I won't keep you long.'

Swift followed him down a dark corridor and into a room which seemed overflowing with children of every conceivable age. In their midst was a plump, greasy-looking woman with fiery eyes.

'This is Mrs. Roland and these are Abdul, Saïd, Abderahman, Mohamed, and Betsy.' Observing Swift's surprised expression, he added: 'We agreed to give the boys Arab names and the girls Anglo-Saxon ones. There's also April and Virginia, but they're both out.'

With this breathless explanation he left Swift and disappeared from the room. Swift now smiled uneasily at each member of the family in turn.

'You have a fine family, Mrs. Roland,' he said, on completing the round.

'Mother not speak English,' replied one of the larger children, who then appeared to translate what he'd said. Mrs. Roland shrugged her shoulders in apparent indifference to his remark and replied in a harsh, grating voice.

'Mother say England a fine country also.'

Swift couldn't help reflecting that if she had indeed said this she could hardly have meant it. Happily Mr. Roland's prompt reappearance saved him further effort at profitless conversation. On the way down to the travel agency, he commended Mr. Roland for his fertility.

'Oh, but you didn't see them all,' Mr. Roland said. 'Several of them were out. By the way, I hope you found Ahmed satisfactory today.'

'Yes; though he soaked me when it came to paying.'

'Not you, Mr. Swift. The long-suffering British taxpayers, maybe, but not you personally. I assure you he'd never have dreamt of overcharging a good friend like yourself, if he hadn't known your own pocket wasn't involved.'

'I still consider he stung me.'

Mr. Roland sighed. 'The Briton abroad always expects to be done down. It's almost a national characteristic. He never pauses to consider the different economic values in the land he's visiting.'

'Phooey!' Swift replied agreeably. 'Anyway, what does the rascal do when he's not chauffeuring a gullible Britisher?'

'He helps me,' Mr. Roland said with quiet malice, 'like the dutiful son he is.'

Swift found his return journey infinitely less exhausting than the outward one, largely due to being spared a further encounter with Marseilles Airport. The 'plane flew direct to Paris, where Orly aerodrome greeted him with such welcome cosmopolitanism as notices in English and a bookstall carrying that day's papers flown over from London.

An hour after landing he took to the air again on the last lap of his odyssey: the short hop from Paris to London, which not infrequently takes less time than the appalling drive which succeeds it from the airport into the heart of the metropolis.

He had emerged from Customs and Immigration and had just stopped to take his first conscious breath of damp, mild English air, when who should step forward but Manton.

'Hello, sir!' he said with the immediate upsurge of pleasure that being unexpectedly met can induce.

'Thought I'd come and pick you up,' Manton said laconically. 'I've got a car outside and we can talk on the way into Town.'

They set off, Manton manoeuvring through the traffic in silence while Swift retold the events of his visit. When he had finished, he asked:

'What's the next move, sir: fetch in the old Negress for questioning?'

'Yes. We'll call on her this evening.'

'I wondered if you might have done so already, sir.'

'No, the A.C. reckoned another twenty-four hours wouldn't hurt, and he thought we ought to await your return in case there was something you hadn't been able to mention on the 'phone yesterday. However, the day's not been altogether wasted. We've been checking hard on this fellow Heath. It's true what he told you about being forced to resign, and it was also, as he said, Mendolia who bribed him and was the cause of it all. He'd undoubtedly have been prosecuted if Lord Droxford hadn't put in a good word for him, and generally helped to get him out of the country by insisting it would be the most sensible and humane way out of the difficulty.'

'Any idea, sir, what motives Lord Droxford had for protecting him?'

'None discovered, apart from genuine altruism. Those who've served longest at West End say he's always ready to help a lame dog. Indeed, there can't be many men who have such a high reputation for fair dealing among their staff. They fall over each other in lauding him.'

'I know, sir, it never really looked like coincidence that all the disappearances were from the same court, but now it's even less likely. Obviously one of the vital links in the organization is right there at West End.'

'You say "organization". But what organization? And organization for that?'

'For getting people out of the country, sir, so that they'll avoid going to prison.'

Manton gave a helpless sigh.

'If only we had news of Cordari. If he never got to Algeria, where *has* he got to? And why's he not been able to keep in touch with us?' Divining that he was still pursuing a line of thought, Swift said nothing. 'The only thing I can think is that after they've been spirited out of the country, they're held in some sort of quarantine so that they can't communicate with the outside world for a time.'

'At any rate, the bit in Cordari's letter about there being a shock in store for us is now explained, sir. He obviously knew when he wrote that he wasn't going to Algeria, but that it would be posted out there as part of a blind.'

'Yes, he was on to something all right when he wrote it. Perhaps he gave himself away. Perhaps . . . perhaps . . . perhaps nuts. Speculation's going to get us nowhere. The sooner we pay our call on Susannah the better.'

Shortly after they'd arrived at the Yard, Swift excused himself and hurried off to telephone. With impatient fingers he dialled Pamela's number and waited. But there was no reply.

Manton decided that they should tackle Susannah at her own place and only 'invite' her to accompany them back to the Yard for more vigorous questioning if the need arose.

It was around half past seven that evening when they turned into Sirena Street and walked with purposeful steps towards No. 28.

Swift kept his eyes skinned for anything remotely significant, but, on the surface at least, everything was placid and unpromisingly normal.

The front door of No. 28 was wide open and they looked down a dark, narrow hall with a flight of stairs at the end.

'Come on, we'll go in. Don't want to attract notice by standing about outside.' Half-way down the hall on the right was a door with a Yale lock on it.

'This is her room, sir,' Swift whispered.

Manton rapped on the door and was immediately rewarded by hearing Susannah's deep answering tones.

'Who's that?'

71

'Open up, Susannah. We've got something important to talk to you about.'

'Who is it?'

'Police.'

'I don't recognize your voice,' she replied suspiciously.

'We're from Scotland Yard, not your local station.'

'How many of you are there?'

'Two.'

'What do you want?'

'We've got something very important to ask you about.'

'Am I in trouble?'

'Not yet. Now, open the door.'

The officers heard her footsteps, then a click and the door swung open. The old Negress stood blocking the entrance and staring sightlessly at them, her eyes looking like two blobs of jelly behind the thick lenses of her spectacles.

Manton made no move, but said quietly: 'May we come in?' He went on to introduce Swift and himself. When he'd finished, Susannah turned and walked to a chair over by the fireplace. It was an old basket one, covered with odd loose pieces of material. She sat down in it and deftly put out a hand to stir the small saucepan that was steaming on a gas-ring beside her.

Manton moved into the centre of the room and Swift closed the door behind them. It was a bed-sitting-room cum kitchen which gave the appearance of having been furnished by an acquisitive jackdaw who specialized in raids on junk shops.

'How long have you lived here?' Manton asked.

'Since nineteen forty-two.'

'You were here all through the air raids?'

'Yes.'

'Is this your only room in the house?'

'Yes.'

'What about bathroom and lavatory?'

'There's a lavatory at the back and a tap in the passage outside it.'

'Who else lives here?'

'People come and go.'

'What sort of people?'

'All sorts, I suppose.'

'Who owns the house?'

It seemed from her expression that Manton might as well have asked her who owned fishing rights on the moon, for she shook her head and gave an impatient shrug. He decided it was now time to get down to the real business of their visit. Watching her intently, he said: 'Just under a fortnight ago, a man disappeared. We think he was smuggled out of the country and that you, wittingly or otherwise, played a part in the matter.' She had ceased stirring the small pan on the gas-ring and was leaning forward in an attitude of alertness. 'Do you want me to go on?' She peered for a moment in his direction and then turned her head away again. It was impossible to read her thoughts. 'This man was told to drop certain coins into your tin when he left court. . . . Now do you know what I'm talking about?'

Susannah cupped her hands together in her lap and bowed her head. There was dignity about all her movements, enhanced in part by contrast with the coarseness of her features. Without a hat, her thick white hair stuck out like wire wool, and something in the pigment of her black skin gave her face a partially scorched appearance.

'Yes; it was a threepenny bit and a halfpenny he gave me,' she said carefully.

'And what did you have to do?'

'Play a certain tune.'

Manton sucked in his breath sharply. So that was it!

'What tune?' he asked.

' "The Desert Song".'

'Did you have to start playing it immediately you heard the two coins go into your tin?'

'No, only when I'd finished what I was playing at the time.'

'You've done it before, haven't you?' She nodded hesitantly. 'Did you ever know who the people were who gave you the money?' This time she shook her head strongly. Manton drew a long breath as he paused on the brink of the most vital question of all. A question to which one answer could almost terminate their inquiry that very night; another send them groping even farther along the dark vale of uncertainty. 'Who were you acting for?'

The answer was immediate, if surprising.

'The man who collects the rent.'

'His name? What's his name?'

Swift thought he saw the trace of a smile flit across the old Negress's face.

'I don't know his name,' she said.

73

'But who owns this house?' Manton asked in an exasperated tone, conscious as he did so that he'd already once failed with this question.

'You've asked that before.' And then as though suddenly conjuring up a vision of her unknown landlord, she added: 'He is a big man; a rich man. He would not be likely to come here himself. He is too important.'

'How do you know?'

'Perhaps that is how I imagine him,' she replied unsatisfactorily.

'And the man who collects the rent, how often does he come?'

'Perhaps every two weeks.'

'Does he collect from everyone in the house?'

'They all pay their rent to me and I pay it to him.'

'And what happens when tenants leave and new ones come?'

'I arrange.' And then as if reading his thoughts she added: 'I know all that goes on in this house.'

'Then you must also know to whom you pay over the money?' Manton pressed.

'That is different.'

'Has it been the same man all the while you've lived here?'

'No, no.'

'And the present one? How long has he been collecting the rent?'

'A long time now. One year, perhaps two years.'

'When did he last call?'

'Two weeks ago, perhaps.'

'And how much did you hand him on that occasion?'

'Forty-two pounds. Always forty-two pounds.'

'Always? Rents not gone up at all in Sirena Street?'

'Forty-two pounds since many months,' she conceded. Then to underline her ill use by the world, she went on: 'Now it is very difficult for poor old blind woman. These new five-pound notes! They try to deceive her. They are too much the same size as one pounds.'

'O.K., so on this last occasion you handed over what? Eight fivers and two one-pound notes, is that it?'

'I give it that way since this new five-pound money come. The man says it is better. For four, five times, I now give it him like that.'

'And was the occasion we're speaking of before or after the

last time you played "The Desert Song" for him?' Manton asked, carefully emphasizing every word.

'It was the day before, I think.'

'So! Was it then he gave you your instructions?'

'He just told me it might happen again the next morning and that the boss would be listening.'

'You mean that someone might drop a threepenny bit and a halfpenny into your tin and you were to play the tune?' She nodded. 'How much were you paid each time?'

'Nothing.'

'What have you got out of it?'

'The boss is kind to an old black woman. He lets me live here cheap. I repay him.'

'I see. How many times have you done this particular thing for him.'

'Four, five, six. I don't remember.'

'What were you told the first time?' He noticed her puzzled expression. 'What reason were you given for being asked to play "The Desert Song"?'

'The man said it would please the boss.'

'And that was good enough for you?'

'Yes.'

He stared hard about him before letting his eyes come back to rest on Susannah.

'You stay here. We're going to have a look over the house.' He motioned to Swift with his head and they went out into the hall. There were two floors above, each of them with three rooms. All were poorly furnished and had a fetid odour. Four were empty. One had a Maltese lying asleep in his underwear on top of an iron bed. The other they never got inside, but startled and protesting sounds from the far side of the door left them in no doubt as to its occupants.

On the ground floor, apart from Susannah's room, was the lavatory and a scum-stained kitchen, both apparently in communal use. A door just past the lavatory led out into a small concrete yard on to which backed the houses in a parallel street.

Satisfied that they had mastered the geography of the premises, the two officers returned to Susannah's room. She was sitting just as they had left her, save that she was now feeding herself from a bowl which she held in her lap.

'Is there a cellar to the house?' Manton asked. He hadn't seen any sign of one, but thought it might have a secret entrance, being aware that most such houses did possess one.

'No cellar.'

'Where did you go during air raids?' he asked in idle curiosity.

'I stayed here. Others went to a shelter at the back.'

'Do you know anything about your near neighbours?'

She shook her head. 'Only Pepito. He also pays his rent to me.'

'Who is Pepito?'

'He has the workshop in Syracuse Street. It is at the back here.'

Soon after this Manton and Swift took their leave of the old Negress, first warning her that she would be under constant surveillance from then on and consequently had better behave herself, or else ... It was all they could do, though Manton doubted the efficacy of threats, in the circumstances.

Outside, Manton scanned the front of the house and those of its neighbours. Between No. 28 and the house on its right ran a narrow passage. Entrance to this was barred by a wooden gate which stood framed by the front walls of the adjoining houses. Manton tried the latch and the gate opened.

'We'd better have a look along here,' he said.

At the far end they could see another gate, which clearly let out into Syracuse Street. The passage ran between two eight-foot brick walls in which the only break was a doorway on the left. It stood about four feet back from the wall-line and was eighteen inches or so below the passage-level. A cement apron sloped down to it. The door was heavily padlocked, and when Manton tried it it was apparent that it was also secured by a further lock.

'That must be the air-raid shelter she mentioned, sir,' Swift said.

Manton nodded. 'Wonder what it's used for now? Just the sort of storehouse for stolen property, by the look of it. We'd better have a squint inside some time.' They moved on down the passage. The gate at the far end was likewise unbolted and they found themselves in Syracuse Street.

Pepito's workshop had a thoroughly dilapidated air about it from the front and appeared to be very largely boarded up. It had a sort of stable-door entrance, which Manton now approached. As he did so, Swift heard faint blacksmith sounds from within.

The occupant of the workshop was a small, thick-set man with a sallow, pock-marked complexion. He was bending over a bench which stood against one of the side walls and which was littered with miscellaneous scraps of machinery.

'You Pepito?' Manton asked.

'Yes,' the man replied in a slow, suspicious tone.

'We're police. We've got a few questions to ask you. Who owns this place?'

'I rent it.'

'From whom?'

Pepito began to show sudden signs of agitation, and in an excited voice said:

'I always pay my rent. I am a good man. I never give no trouble.'

'O.K., then there's no need to get excited. All I want to know is from whom you rent the place?'

'I do not have dealings with the owner. I do not even know who he is. I pay the money to Susannah, the old black girl who lives in Sirena Street. She gives it to a man.' Defiantly he added: 'There is nothing against the law in that.'

'What do you do here?' Manton asked.

'Small engineering jobs and metal cleaning. It is an honest business. I am never in trouble.'

Manton pretended not to notice his agitation.

'Know anything about the shelter at the back?'

Pepito started so obviously that both officers at once looked at him with a new alertness.

'It is not mine. I have nothing to do with it. I have never been in there. It is locked. I know nothing.' The sentences rattled out in stammering volubility and were followed by a silence in which Pepito, now looking thoroughly scared, rolled his eyes from one to the other of the officers, who in their turn stared back in thoughtful appraisal. It was Swift who spoke.

'It may not be yours. You may have nothing to do with it. You may never have been in there; but you quite definitely do know something. What is it?'

'I have done nothing against the law.'

'Stop whimpering and tell us what you know?'

'A man uses it occasionally. I do not know him and he is not there very often, I think. I have never seen him there. He has sometimes sent me messages and I have only ordered things for him and left them outside the door. That is all I know. It is the whole truth.'

'What sort of things have you ordered for him?' Manton asked quietly.

The question seemed to cause Pepito deeper anguish. Eventually, however, he threw out a despairing arm and pointed towards the far corner of the workshop. Like two ravens of ill omen, Manton and Swift slowly turned their heads. There, each with its glass neck sticking primly out of a protective straw nest, stood six large carboys of acid.

Swift was all for getting Pepito to force the shelter door for them immediately, but Manton insisted that they must first get a search-warrant.

'However, don't fret—we can get one without delay,' he said. 'We don't have to wait for a court in the morning. We'll apply at once to one of the magistrates at his home. Not to Lord Droxford, though,' he added decidedly.

Within an hour and a half they had their search-warrant, also a bunch of skeleton keys. Watch had meanwhile been maintained and no one had gone near the shelter nor even used the passage which gave access to it.

While Manton had been away seeing about getting the warrant, Swift, who had been busy reconnoitring, had discovered that the Syracuse Street entrance to the passage was no more than two hundred yards from the point where Cordari had vanished in Derry Street. On Manton's return, he pointed this out and then with pent-up excitement set about opening the door. This proved a relatively simple task. It was flung open, however, only to reveal a tiny lobby, with another locked door between them and the main part of the premises. Swift worked away at the inner door to a series of muttered prayers and curses. At last the right key was found and there was a rewarding click as he turned it.

The room inside was quite dark and he felt down the side of the wall for a switch.

'Here, I'll strike a match,' Manton said. A moment later the light had been turned on. At first sight the room appeared virtually bare. It was rectangular with a low ceiling and four plain white-washed walls. Over in one corner was a plain wooden table and a chair. Along the wall on the right was an alcove which was curtained off, and it was this that first attracted their attention. Manton walked over and drew the curtain aside.

The sight which met their eyes was as sinister as it was revealing. Two empty carboys stood beside a large oil drum, the bottom of which, when the cover was removed, showed traces of thick sludge. Near the drum was an open drain with heavy staining on the stone floor around it. And jutting out from the wall was a tap with a short length of hosepipe neatly coiled over it.

Quite suddenly Swift felt that he wanted to vomit. Manton, too, hardened though he was, stared with a sort of mesmerized horror at the gaping drain.

At length, in a dull, shocked tone, he said:

'So this is where they were brought—and murdered.'

CHAPTER FIFTEEN

Swift was the first to turn away from the scene; a scene that was so utterly sickening in all it suggested. There seemed small room for doubt that Cordari and the six men who had disappeared before him had got no nearer to Algeria than this shelter; that they had been lured here and killed in nauseous circumstances, their remains being poured down a drain like so much swill.

Slowly the first impact began to wear off and he fell to wondering who could have been capable of such inhumanity: what part had been played by the mysterious figure who, grimly and silently, had slid out of the shadows of Derry Street that night and claimed Cordari?

Manton, now, also turned back into the room. His face was grey and there was an odd stiffness in his movements.

'It's pretty horrible, isn't it?' Then in a slow, thoughtful tone, he added: 'There was a man in France a few years ago who murdered Iron Curtain refugees after promising to fix them up with false papers and get them out of Europe. He used to impress on them the necessity for secrecy, and then when they reported for their journey he bumped them off and made himself rich on their possessions. And being refugees, of course, they'd usually converted everything they owned into jewellery

79

or hard currency, which made it a nice, easy harvest for him. Afterwards, I think, he either burnt or melted down their bodies.'

'Do you imagine that's what's been happening here, sir?'

But Manton appeared lost in thought again and didn't reply, his eyes roaming the shelter. Apart from the table and chair in the corner, the only other furniture, if such it could be called, was a row of bare coat-hooks on the wall. It was not these, however, that now claimed his attention. Noticing the line of his gaze, Swift looked in the same direction.

'Looks like a pair of rubber boots under the table,' Manton said. 'Fish them out. But for God's sake be careful not to touch the outsides; they may have prints on them.'

Swift retrieved the boots and stood them in the middle of the floor. Then picking up the left one by thrusting his arm inside, he swivelled it around for inspection.

'These were obviously worn by the murderer,' Manton said. 'You can see that from the stains on the welt and sole—also by where the acid has begun to eat into the rubber.'

'If they were worn by a man, sir, he must have had unusually small feet,' Swift observed.

'A murderer with small feet,' Manton said reflectively. Once more he gazed slowly about him, his eyes coming finally back to the boots. 'The first thing will be to try to discover who made them and where they were bought.' He turned to go. 'Come on, we must get cracking.'

Soon after half past nine the next morning, P.C. Tredgold and Arnold Plowman, the usher, were working at opposite ends of a long table in the hinter-region of the jailer's office at West End Court. Tredgold was checking details of the morning's cases in Lord Droxford's large register and Plowman was sorting mail. Without looking up, Tredgold said:

'Remember I told you last week, Arnold, that one of those defendants who absconded on bail was really a Yard officer who was trying to find out what was happening? Well, all hell's broken loose since last night. They think they've got evidence that all of them have been murdered in some disused shelter off Sirena Street and it seems they're taking the place apart brick by brick.'

'Go on!' Plowman exclaimed with interest.

'Yes. They've practically had the Commissioner himself there.

As it is, scores of C.I.D. boys are milling around, so I hear, while the Director of the lab. and one of the pathologists have been scooping out the drains.'

'Sounds more like they need a good plumber.'

'Whatever they need. I don't envy the chap who's knocked off a copper.'

'It's certainly the surest way of bringing the whole bloody hornet's nest about your head,' Plowman agreed. He rose and carefully picked up the small piles of mail he'd arranged on the table. 'Well, I'd better deliver this lot.'

'How are things at home? Any better?' Tredgold asked as the usher was about to go.

Plowman paused and made a face.

'Between you and me, my wife's a bitch and nothing'll ever change her,' he said, without apparent malice.

Tredgold shook his head in mute sympathy and continued to do so after Plowman's departure. He felt sorry for the usher; for that matter for anyone who hadn't got a plump, placid, uncomplaining Mrs. Tredgold for a wife. It was remarkable, really, he reflected, how cheerful Plowman managed to keep in the circumstances.

Plowman, meanwhile, climbed the stairs to the short corridor where Lord Droxford and Mr. Astbury had their respective rooms. He heard the sound of voices coming from Lord Droxford's and waited a moment before knocking.

When he did knock, there was an immediate 'Come in.' He entered to find both Mr. Astbury and Mr. Rex Turnbull with the magistrate. They had ceased their discussion when the door opened and now watched him with ill-concealed impatience as he handed Lord Droxford his mail.

'Only one for you this morning, sir,' he said. It was a letter which bore the postmark 'Ourasa' and, in bold red letters, was labelled 'Express.'

A momentary frown of annoyance furrowed Lord Droxford's brow as he took it. Then placing it quickly upside down on his desk, he nodded dismissal at Plowman and turned to resume his conversation with the other two men.

Having been up the whole of the night, Swift slipped off duty at about half past seven for a quick shave and some breakfast. But before he attended to either of these matters he 'phoned Pamela. An extremely sleepy voice answered.

'Pamela, this is Kevin. I've got to see you. Something very important's happened.'

Her voice sounded immediately wide awake and she said quickly: 'Ah, you're back! Any news of Roy?'

'I'll tell you about everything when we meet,' he replied guardedly.

An hour later Swift arrived at the rendezvous, a new Espresso bar just off Regent Street, and chose a secluded table over in a corner. The bar's contrast with the awful shelter from which he'd come could hardly have been more marked. It was gay and bright, with the latest in functional decoration.

As soon as Pamela arrived, he fetched from the counter two cups of coffee in which dollops of fleecy white cream gently dissolved.

'When did you get back?' she asked as he manoeuvred round their table like a juggler.

'Yesterday afternoon. I tried to ring you, but I couldn't get a reply.'

'I was out.'

'With Mendolia?'

'Yes,' she replied, quickly brushing aside the question. 'What's happened to Roy?'

With difficulty and in halting language, Swift related the events of the past eighteen hours. When he had finished there was a painful silence, in which she sat quite motionless, staring down into her lap.

'Of course, it's not yet been possible to identify any of the ...' He hesitated, and added in a tone of quiet misery: '... of the remains.'

'Do you think they ever will be able to?'

'It's very doubtful. It depends.' As he spoke, there floated again before his mind's eye a vision of the small grim particles he had seen painstakingly recovered by Dr. Anselm, the pathologist, from the iron drum and the walls of the drain itself—all that now remained of a vital human body; a body which was now no more; a body whose only relics might be an insoluble kidney-stone, a piece of denture, a chip of bone and, above all, a mass of nauseating, yellow grease. From some of these finds they might eventually be able to identify one of the hapless victims. Scientific detection was in its golden age and made a point of frequently achieving the seemingly impossible. But, however that might be, it was now irresistibly clear that the shelter had been not only the scene of murder but of the murder of those elusive defendants who had defied West End Court; and of Detective Constable Roy Cordari, a proud and worthy member of the Metropolitan Police.

'Nobody's yet broken the news to Doreen, have they?' Pamela asked, her voice carefully controlled. Swift shook his head and stretched out a hand and sought hers. He gently stroked it, for a moment incapable of speech. 'Are there any clues to the murderer?'

'There may be. It's too early to say. But there aren't any obvious ones.' In a fiercer tone, he added: 'But nobody's going to rest till we've got him and avenged Roy's death. And you must help us.'

Staring across the room with unseeing eyes, Pamela spoke in a voice strange to Swift's ears.

'I swear I will. Whoever he is, I want to see him on the end of a rope.'

Swift caressed her hand soothingly. There was something almost frightening in the intensity of her emotion. So much so that it wasn't till some time later that he was able to think back clearly on all that had passed between them.

'I must go in a minute,' he said, and fished in his pocket for some loose change. 'Have you found out anything about Mendolia while I've been away?'

Pamela bit her lip nervously. 'No; I don't think he's mixed up in——' She broke off suddenly and said: 'Anyway, surely this latest news completely knocks out your theory of a smuggling organization.'

'Mr. Manton still thinks it's likely that the murders were the product of a gang racket, though not necessarily the sort of racket we originally imagined.'

'What racket was it, then?'

'Gangs have been known to go in for murder for a number of different reasons,' Swift replied, a trifle uncomfortably.

'And you still believe that Mendolia's mixed up in this?'

He stared distantly into his empty coffee cup. Then looking up, he met Pamela's gaze. 'Whatever's the answer to that, you're the one who can find out. Even if Mendolia wasn't directly concerned, it happened right in his territory and he's bound to know something.'

Soon after Swift and Pamela Stoughton had left the coffee

shop and parted company, Joe Mendolia stepped out of his Jaguar, walked briskly across the pavement and mounted the stairs that led up to Mr. Rex Turnbull's offices. The girl behind the inquiry desk greeted him deferentially and conducted him immediately to the solicitor's room. This faced the entrance of West End Court and enabled his clerk on really hectic days to communicate the state of the court's business by standing outside and waving his arms like a tic-tac man. In contrast with the rest of the premises, it was sumptuously furnished.

Mendolia walked across and seated himself in the easy chair which stood at one end of Mr. Turnbull's desk. It was low-slung and gave Mr. Turnbull the psychological edge of being able to look down on his clients. He knew, however, that this didn't work with Joe Mendolia.

'Still prospering, Rex?' Mendolia said with an amused smile, gazing around him. 'That's a new picture you've got on the wall over there, isn't it?'

'Only a reproduction,' Mr. Turnbull said primly, in refutation of any implied charge of extravagance.

'I gather half the rozzers in London are buzzing round Sirena Street this morning,' Mendolia said quizzically, swinging his gaze slowly back to the desk where Mr. Turnbull sat watching him. 'Seems somebody has been going in for murder on a grand scale. Least, that's what I've picked up. You heard the same?'

'Yes, they were talking about it when I was over at court earlier this morning.'

'Who's in charge of the investigation?'

'One of the Yard superintendents. Manton, I think.'

'Isn't he the one who's been trying to dig up something about those defendants who jumped their bail? Is it true also that one of his officers has vanished?'

'I have heard rumours to that effect,' Mr. Turnbull said with a lawyer's caution. He gave his visitor a slightly wintry smile. 'Happily you don't own anything in Sirena Street, so there's no need for you to worry.'

'Quite true; and now I'll tell you what I've really come to see you about.' Mendolia recrossed his legs and leaned indolently back. 'I may be going abroad soon.'

'What's remarkable about that? Quite a lot of people seem to, from what I hear,' Mr. Turnbull observed dryly. 'Is it business or pleasure, or one of those popular combinations of both, that you're contemplating?'

'I don't mean just for a while. I mean for good.'

This time Mr. Turnbull's features did give him away, though he recovered himself quickly.

'Leaving England for good?' he echoed. 'This is very sudden, isn't it? And where are you proposing to go?'

Mendolia smiled at him with amusement.

'I'm not really sure yet,' he said thoughtfully. 'But I'd like you to apply your mind to the question so that when my plans are a bit more definite you can give me some good advice on what to do about my interest here.'

'But . . . but . . . but I can't possibly begin to advise you until I know more,' Mr. Turnbull expostulated. 'I mean, it'll depend on where you're going, and whether you want to sell up completely—oh, and a host of other considerations.'

'Don't fuss, Rex, I'll let you know all that in due course. Meanwhile, just turn it over in your mind. On the basis, say, that I shall probably want to realize all my assets. And then if I don't, well, no harm's done and you can readjust your ideas.'

'You're not likely to be going off suddenly; without proper notice?' Mr. Turnbull asked suspiciously.

Mendolia threw back his head and laughed delightedly.

'Doing a glorified midnight flit, you mean? No, not me. Why, I'll even have it announced in advance in the columns of the *Police Gazette*!'

With animal grace he rose from the visitors' chair, straightened his tie and brushed a few specks of dust from the lapels of his smartly tailored light-grey suit. At the door, he turned back and said:

'I'll let you know just as soon as I can.'

On his way out, he passed Manton, who was making an unheralded call on the solicitor. The two men paused as they drew level on the staircase.

' 'Morning, Super,' Mendolia said cheerfully. 'Hear you've got a real plateful. However, I reckon it's going to be too bad for someone. Everyone knows you never let go when one of your own boys is involved. Bloody silly to think of doing in a copper.'

'And just rotten luck of course, if it was all a big mistake, and the someone wasn't aware of his identity,' Manton said caustically.

Mendolia cocked his head on one side and appeared to ponder the comment seriously. Then he gave a slight shrug as though to indicate that this was the ineluctable way of the world and passed on down.

A few moments later, Manton was ushered into Mr. Turn-bull's office. Just before he sat down in the recently vacated chair, he took a quick look out of the window and was in time to see Mendolia's car do a wide U-turn in the street and drive off towards the heart of Soho. As it did so, Susannah at her usual post outside the entrance to West End Court raised her voice in Delilah's most well-known of all songs from Saint-Saëns's opera. He had heard her sing it before and had been struck by the raw beauty of her voice. It was a contralto's perfect showpiece.

'Doesn't it get on your nerves having a permanent musical accompaniment to your work?' he asked, fixing Mr. Turnbull with a pleasant stare.

'Hardly ever notice it now, except when someone draws attention to the old girl, as you've just done.' As he spoke, he doodled at the side of his blotter. 'However, what is it you think I can do for you, Superintendent? I've got to go over to court soon, so perhaps you'd state your business straight away.'

Manton nodded. 'Yes, of course. You probably know that I'm investigating the disappearance of a number of defendants from West End Court who skipped their bail and haven't been heard of since. The reason I've come to see you is that I think I'm right in saying that you appeared for each of them—or at least for all but one.' Mr. Turnbull said nothing and Manton fished an envelope out his jacket pocket and consulted the back. 'There was Skourasi, who vanished about a fortnight ago. A man called Brufa, some time last month. And before him there were Vapilos, Apel, Plaxides, Averoff and Osuna. They've all disappeared within the last six months, and there's good reason to believe that they were in fact murdered soon after they disappeared. That being the case, I'd be glad if you'd tell me anything you can about them.'

'I certainly don't see why not. But let me put one matter in its proper perspective. I have by far and away the largest single advocate's practice at West End—anyone over there'll confirm that for you—and so the fact that these men whose disappearances you're investigating were mostly clients of mine is no more than a very slight coincidence.'

'I'm quite prepared to accept that,' Manton said blandly, adding to himself: 'for the time being, at any rate.' Unseen by him, Mr. Turnbull had pressed a bell, for the door suddenly opened and a trim-looking female of indefinite age stood there.

'You rang, Mr. Turnbull?'

'Yes, Miss Allison. Would you please bring me the files of Skourasi, Brufa, Vapilos, Apel, Plaxides and Averoff. You know the clients who——'

'Oh, those pending-trial files, you mean,' she interrupted, in an exasperatingly efficient tone. 'I'll get them for you right away, Mr. Turnbull.'

'Worth her weight in gold, and every bit as competent as she thinks she is. In fact, the only indispensable member of the staff. Incidentally, the last name you mentioned is the one that doesn't belong in my pack.'

'As far as I can find out he wasn't legally represented at all,' Manton said.

'Most unwise,' Mr. Turnbull said solemnly.

In next to no time Miss Allison had returned and deposited a pile of buff-coloured folders in front of her employer.

'They're in chronological order again now,' she said with an admonitory air. Mr. Turnbull murmured his thanks.

'Now let's see,' he said, opening the top one. While Manton sat quietly listening, the solicitor proceeded to read out a string of details concerning his late clients. These consisted for the greater part of their full names, their addresses, their occupations and particulars of the offences with which they'd been charged. When he came to the last file, he looked across at Manton and said sardonically: 'Do you want to have Mr. Skourasi's particulars too—or may we take them as read?'

'When did you first learn that Skourasi was really a police officer?'

'I heard rumours over at the court a few days ago. I think it was someone in the jailer's office who was talking about it. Probably Tredgold, but I can't be sure.'

Manton nodded his head slowly and tried to look intelligent, though in fact his brain was beginning to reel from lack of sleep, aided by the lulling effect of Mr. Turnbull's voice. Clenching his jaw muscles to stifle a yawn, he said:

'There is one question I'd like to ask you about these clients of yours. Did all of them appear to be fairly well off for money?'

'I think I can say "yes" to that,' Mr. Turnbull replied carefully.

87

'Apart from the money which they paid you, you got the impression there was lots more where it came from?'

'None of them seemed to be short. I'm not saying they were millionaires, mind you, but—er—they certainly didn't seem to be embarrassed by their legal costs.'

'A tribute to your reasonable charges, I'm sure.'

'No doubt,' Mr. Turnbull observed dryly, restacking, with exaggerated care, the files Miss Allison had produced. He looked ostentatiously out of the window and then at his watch. 'And now, if you'll excuse me, Superintendent, I must be getting across to court.' He rose from his desk. 'We're awfully lucky here, you know. Couldn't be a pleasanter court to work in. Everyone from Lord Droxford down is always ready to help. Can't be many others where there's such a congenial atmosphere.'

Manton, who'd also got up, shook himself and joined him over by the door.

'And further sweetened by music,' he said.

'Yes, old Susannah's very much one of us,' the solicitor agreed heartily.

'How long has she been there?'

'Almost longer than I care to remember. Certainly over twenty years. Tough old girl, too! She hardly misses a day. Just occasionally in very bad weather nowadays she'll not appear.'

The two men left the premises together. Outside on the pavement Mr. Turnbull said:

'Give me a call if there's anything else you want to know. Meanwhile, good hunting.'

Manton watched him cross the road and disappear into the court building. A moment later, after a reflective pause he followed him over. Making straight for the jailer's office, he pushed his way through the usual crowd of police officers and defendants who thronged there and went straight up to P.C. Tredgold.

'Can I have a quiet word with you?'

Tredgold looked round the office and sighed.

'O.K. sir,' he said. 'I'll just ask Sergeant Topham to hold the fort.' This done, he led the way along the corridor where the cells were. 'Here's an empty one. This'll be as quiet as anywhere.'

'Do you remember Heath, the late usher here?' Manton asked as soon as they were seated on the cell's hard wooden bench.

'Gordon Heath? Yes, I remember him all right, sir.'

'He had to resign, didn't he?'

'That's right. It was bad luck in a way. He was let down by that crook Mendolia, but of course he never ought to have got himself into the position in the first place. Drink and women, they were his weaknesses. Extraordinary how often they go together.'

'He passed some police information to Mendolia. Wasn't that it?'

Tredgold nodded his head.

'Yes, and then Mr. Turnbull used it in court and there was one hell of a rumpus. Never have been able to feel quite the same about Mr. Turnbull since then, though I suppose it wasn't really his fault. He was only doing what his client paid him to do. But it was the sort of thing that left a nasty taste in the mouth, if you know what I mean, sir.'

'And is it true that Lord Droxford came to Heath's rescue?'

P.C. Tredgold's expression softened as he replied:

'There's a real gentleman for you. Not many of his sort left nowadays. He not only saved Heath from possible prosecution—though, mark you, I doubt whether they could have proved a charge of bribery against him in court—but he helped him to get away and live abroad. Suffered awful with his chest, Heath did, 'specially when there was any fog about.'

'Has anyone heard anything of him since he left?'

'I believe he's kept in touch with Lord Droxford. A letter at Christmas and that sort of thing. He'd have shown a darned lack of gratitude if he hadn't.'

'What kind of fellow was he really?'

'He was all right, except for being a bit weak, as I've told you. He did his job O.K. and got on with everyone well enough.'

Manton stared thoughtfully at the plain tiled walls of the cell. Tredgold's picture of the ex-usher certainly conformed with that brought back by Swift. Namely that Heath had been no more than the supine agent of an unknown murderer right here in London.

If Tredgold's curiosity was aroused by Manton's interest in the man, he forbore to show it as he sat stolidly awaiting the next question. He was an officer of the old régime who worked on the theory that his superiors would tell him all they wanted him to know and it wasn't for him to be inquisitive.

'How well do you know Joe Mendolia?' Manton asked suddenly.

'Sufficiently to look upon him as a thoroughly undesirable type. Smart, mind you, and not without—well, a coating of charm, though I begrudge the use of that word to describe him.'

'I should think rumour's done a good deal to inflate his shadow, hasn't it?'

'Could be,' Tredgold said after a pause. 'I agree one's apt to accept as a matter of course that he's behind practically every racket in this area.'

'Has he any reputation for violence that you know of?'

'He's never been up for violence himself, but one or two of his thug-boys have on the odd occasion.'

Manton had some time ago found out from the Criminal Record Office that Mendolia had no official record for violence, but he wanted to know whether this was through innocence or failure to get caught. It seemed to be the former.

'Has he any moral scruples?'

P.C. Tredgold now looked at him with something approaching astonishment, and Manton, realizing how curious his question must have sounded in the circumstances, added quickly: 'I mean, is he capable of murder; or at any rate of a racket involving murder?'

'I don't see why not,' the jailer replied, while his mind still sniffed suspiciously at 'moral scruples'. From all accounts Superintendent Manton was a good officer as well as being a nice man, but times had certainly changed since the day he, Tredgold, had joined the Metropolitan Police. One wouldn't have heard a senior officer of that period asking whether a C.R.O. man had 'moral scruples'. But then there weren't all these psychiatrists in those days, either, Tredgold reflected with a short-lived gleam of satisfaction.

Manton thanked him for his help and together they returned to the hubbub of the office. On his way out of the building, he passed through the court and stood for a moment or two listening to Mr. Turnbull, who was pleading for a sorry-looking client whose right arm was in a sling and whose head was so enveloped in bandages that one puffy eye and a pair of swollen lips were all that appeared. He was a centre of interest, amused and cynical, which became comprehensible to Manton only on learning that he was charged with assaulting, when truculently drunk the previous night, a police officer of singularly robust appearance.

Amusement was increased when Lord Droxford let the man go, with the comment that he'd best keep off drink if it led him to pick such unsuitable sparring partners.

As the man limped out of court, Plowman caught Manton's eye and gave him a knowing wink. Hoisting his black gown higher on to his shoulders, he sauntered over.

'Ever seen anyone quite so done up like a steak-and-kidney pudding?' he asked with a chuckle. 'How's the inquiry going? Hear you've a got a real sticky one on your hands.' Before he could go on, however, Mr. Astbury's severest voice interrupted.

'Could we have a little less noise in court?'

'Silence!' shouted Plowman, glaring hard in the direction of the public gallery.

Manton slipped out quickly. He paused on the pavement and cocked an ear in Susannah's direction to recognize the catchy theme from 'The Threepenny Opera'. It sounded melodiously innocent, but he'd now almost got to suspecting that everything she played had some hidden significance. But for whom? Could it be for the someone whose feet fitted the mysterious pair of boots left in the shelter? Though careful, surreptitious glances at the extremities of those people he'd been talking to that morning had told him nothing.

On Manton's instructions, Swift was spending the morning trying to discover who was the owner of 28 Sirena Street.

His first call was at the local Town Hall, where he hoped the rating list would reveal the answer. But a sight of this was apparently much easier sought than achieved.

The first official to whom he stated his mission listened in stony silence and then disappeared, only to return with another to whom everything had to be explained again from the beginning.

'I don't think I can let you look at our files,' the second official said with a pout. 'They're confidential, you see.'

'But this is an urgent police matter.'

'I dare say, but regulations are regulations. And supposing I let you, what am I then going to say when others ask to see them?'

I don't know and I care still less, was the reply Swift felt inclined to make. But he realized he must exhibit patience—at least for a time yet.

'But Mr.—er——'

'Pilkley.'

'All right, Mr. Pilkley, don't show me the list if it's against the rules, just tell me who's the owner of Number Twenty-eight Sirena Street.'

'That really amounts to the same thing, doesn't it? You're still asking me to break the regulations.' Mr. Pilkley's tongue fished energetically around his teeth. 'I'll tell you what I suggest you do.' His hand dived under the counter and came up holding a form. 'Take this away and complete it, setting out very fully in this bottom panel the exact reasons for which you request the information, then post it back and it'll receive attention.'

'After passing through all the usual channels, I suppose?'

'It must do that, of course.'

With slow deliberation, Swift crumpled the form until it was something the size of a ping-pong ball. Then he tossed it casually on to the counter between them.

'I have no intention of filling up any of your forms, Mr. Pilkley,' he ground out. 'But what I shall do is return to the Yard and make sure that before ever you get sipping your mid-morning cup of tea every officer from the Commissioner down knows that a certain Mr. Pilkley is deliberately obstructing the police in a murder inquiry on the grounds that——'

'Now come, come, there's no need to carry on like that,' Mr. Pilkley broke in hastily, looking distinctly flushed and bothered, but yet with a gleam of hope in his eye. 'You never said anything about murder before. That makes it rather different. Mind you, it'll still be against regulations, but I think perhaps we may be able to manage something after all. Now if I asked you to wait in my office a few moments and while I was out of the room you happened to see the ledger on my desk . . .'

Though Swift managed to stifle the comment that rose to his lips, he had no intention of letting Mr. Pilkley off as easily as that.

'Where is your office?' he asked brusquely. Mr. Pilkley lifted the flap of the counter to let him pass and then led the way through a door with a frosted glass panel and down a green-tiled corridor to the end room on the left.

Whistling nervously to himself, he fetched from a cupboard a large ledger which he placed on his desk and thumbed open at the index letter 'S'. As Swift put out a hand for it, Mr. Pilkley gave a distracted squeak and hurried out of the room, closing the door firmly behind him.

It took Swift less than a minute to find the information he required. The ratepayer of 28 Sirena Street was shown as 'Susannah Nehemials, Occupier.'

This was what he had half feared; namely, that the real owner wasn't likely in the circumstances, to have disclosed himself to the local authority. He quickly flicked over several pages of the ledger until he came to the list of ratepayers in Syracuse Street. Opposite No. 56, which was Pepito's workshop, there appeared 'Susannah Nehemials, Occupier of 28 Sirena Street'.

He closed the book and went out into the corridor. Almost immediately Mr. Pilkley popped out of an adjoining room, his expression an anxious question mark.

'I want to know whether the rates for Fifty-six Syracuse Street and Twenty-eight Sirena Street are normally paid by cheque or in cash,' Swift said in a tone that brooked no demur.

Mr. Pilkley scurried back into his own room and bent over his desk.

'Cash. Always cash,' he answered, as though expecting the heavens to break.

Swift accepted the information with a nod and departed. Clearly the next place to try and dig out the identity of the mysterious owner was the tax office, for here there would certainly be records showing who was responsible for meeting the dues levied on the property by the State.

As he made his way there he contemplated the reception he was likely to get.

He was aware that Government departments were inclined to be monolithically indifferent to the police, and often to each other for that matter, and that intimidation was unlikely to produce results.

It was therefore with some surprise that he found himself being escorted along to a Mr. Wimbush's office within a short time of stating his business. From the reverential tone in which this gentleman's name was mentioned Swift gathered that he was an official of some importance, and this was confirmed, on arrival, by the size of the office, the thickness of the carpet and the superior quality of the furniture. Here were none of the utility trappings of a junior Government employee. Looking at Mr. Wimbush, it was impossible to believe he had ever belonged elsewhere. Thin but dignified and with a coldly reserved manner, he gazed at Swift as though he might have been a well-known tax-evader.

'You want some information about the owner of a certain property, I understand?'

Swift cleared his throat.

'That's right, sir.'

'In connection with some murder you're investigating?' Swift nodded. 'You have your warrant card with you, I take it?'

Swift pulled out his wallet and extracted the document which officially identified him as an officer of the Metropolitan Police. Mr. Wimbush studied it with slow deliberation.

'You understand that the information you request is confidential and not allowed to be divulged except in certain specified circumstances which we need not consider, since they don't arise in this case?'

When he'd got rid of this mouthful, he stared penetratingly at Swift, who squirmed in his chair. Not with embarrassment, but with impatience at the man's devious approach.

'Are you saying, sir, that you're not prepared to give me the information I want?' he asked.

For answer, Mr. Wimbush picked up the telephone receiver and asked for an extension at Scotland Yard. Swift stared stonily at the floor as he listened to a check being made that his business was indeed authentic.

When he replaced the receiver, Mr. Wimbush peered at him through his rimless spectacles and said primly:

'We had an unfortunate experience a few years ago in connection with a murder investigation and so we have to be particularly careful.'

Swift tried to convey by his look that not only was he utterly unmoved by Mr. Wimbush's previous experiences, but that he'd do his damndest to ensure he had another unfortunate one if he didn't co-operate now. It was only later that he learnt that the unfortunate experience referred to had been an imperial blast from a High Court judge who formed the opinion in a certain case (rather unfairly, be the truth known) that Mr. Wimbush, the Government official if not the person, had tried to obstruct the course of justice. It had never amounted to more than some wholly routine pettifogging; but Mr. Wimbush had been left seared, resentful, and determined not to get caught in the fall-out zone a second time.

Mr. Wimbush moved a long tapering finger across his desk

towards a small bell button and pressed it. An inner door to his office opened and a middle-aged female came in holding a file.

'Oh, it's been got out already, has it?' he said, clearly a trifle nonplussed by its prompt appearance, for it was now quite apparent to Swift that the file must have been fetched before even he reached Mr. Wimbush's office. Mr. Wimbush handled it with the gentle care due a precious manuscript.

'You do understand, don't you, that none of the information I give you must be used officially. In court, I mean, without the service of a subpoena.'

To Swift, this was a meaningless formula devised by Mr. Wimbush merely to propitiate his official conscience. He contented himself, however, with a brisk nod and watched the long fingers start to turn the pages of the file. For some time there was silence, as Mr. Wimbush, with cheeks sucked in, burrowed among the sheaf of documents before him. From time to time he would turn back and re-study one with a frown. It all seemed very unnecessary for the one small piece of information Swift had requested. Indeed, he wondered whether the name he wanted wasn't on the face of the file all the time.

'According to our records, the person responsible for declaring this property in his tax return is a Mr. da Suva—Anthony da Suva,' Mr. Wimbush said, closing the file suddenly and looking up.

Swift jotted the name down in his notebook after asking for it to be spelt.

'Of what address?' he continued, pencil poised to write again.

'Of Twenty-eight Sirena Street.'

'But, but . . . are you sure?'

'I can only tell you what we have in our records,' Mr. Wimbush replied icily.

'But no such person lives at that address.'

Mr Wimbush shrugged as if to indicate that wasn't his worry.

'How long has this Mr. da Suva been the owner of the property according to your paper, sir?'

'Four years.'

'And before him?'

Rather unwillingly Mr. Wimbush reopened the file.

'Mr. William Bainter,' he said, and then, as though in answer to Swift's unasked question, added: 'who died intestate in February nineteen fifty-three.'

'Can you tell me about Fifty-six Syracuse Street too?'

'There's a cross-reference in this file showing that the same Mr. da Suva owns it—or rather pays the tax on it.'

'That means ownership, doesn't it?'

'In ninety-nine cases out of a hundred, yes.'

'And this is going to be the hundredth, I know,' Swift commented forlornly.

Finally he thanked Mr. Wimbush for his assistance and parted from him in a spirit of amity such as could scarcely have been foreseen in the earlier moments of their meeting.

While Swift was still wrestling with officialdom, Manton had returned to the shelter.

On his instructions, the passage which joined Sirena and Syracuse Street had been sealed off at each end. Word had got around, however, and a hard core of gawking spectators hovered like vultures to watch all the comings and goings, a special flutter of interest being reserved for the mysterious boxes and containers which, from time to time, were carried out and loaded into waiting police vehicles.

Manton shoved his way past the crowd that surrounded the Sirena Street entrance and through the gate which a uniformed sergeant held open for him. Apart from plugging the entrances to the passage itself, he'd also deemed it necessary to have guards posted at 28 Sirena Street and 56 Syracuse Street. This was done largely to keep the more zealous newspaper reporters at a safe distance.

When he arrived at the shelter, he found Sergeant Talper there alone, standing in the centre of the bare floor rather like the vendor of a house after the removal men have been at work.

'Hello, sir. I think we've almost finished here now. There isn't a square inch that hasn't been photographed and examined.'

And so indeed it appeared. Where the drain had been there was now a yawning hole in the floor, an elaborate plumbing operation having enabled a whole vital section of the original channel to be removed for laboratory examination. Every single stain on walls and floor had been first photographed and then carefully cut away or scraped off and deposited in a labelled container. In all, the police had gone their job with the thoroughness of a trail of driver ants. Talper went on:

'I suppose it's going to be some time before Dr. Anselm or the lab. people can tell us anything definite?'

'Even then, I doubt whether it'll be anything we haven't already guessed.'

'What's your view, sir: that the victims were brought straight here after being picked up, and killed immediately?'

Manton nodded. 'As soon as they'd had time to write a farewell letter, which I imagine they were told would be posted in Algiers when they'd safely be somewhere quite different.'

Sergeant Talper scratched his head in a ruminative sort of way. 'It must have been like a Grand Guignol scene. There was the poor blighter thinking he was about to be got safely out of the country and all the time over in that alcove hidden by a curtain was his execution chamber.' Though a normally stolid West Countryman who in over a quarter of a century's service with the Metropolitan Police had inevitably witnessed a good deal of sudden death, he was still given to short flights of morbid fancy when confronted by something really stark.

'Presumably they were knocked out and killed before being dragged over to the alcove,' Manton replied. After a pause, he added: 'Even this murderer can't have been so inhuman as to try to dissolve live bodies in acid.'

'There weren't any obvious blood-stains around, sir, which looks as though he may have poisoned them first.'

'Could be. A quick lethal toast to a safe journey after the victim had unsuspectingly written his letter.'

'Incidentally, sir, there were quite a few ink-stains on the table that was over in the corner,' Talper said. 'I had it sent along to the lab. with all the other stuff.'

'Good,' Manton replied with an abstracted air. Then reverting to their previous topic he said: 'Of course he may have killed them some other way and cleaned up any mess afterwards. He had a tap and hose.'

'For that matter, sir, there're all sorts of ways of murdering someone without either poisoning them or making a messy job of it. He could have stunned them and then strangled them. He could have suffocated them, chloroformed them——'

'Wait a moment, Andy,' Manton broke in. 'I'm just trying to think . . . yes, that's right, they were all on the small side.' He looked keenly at Talper. 'Whether or not it's significant, I don't know, but it is a fact that each of the missing men was below average height and weight. Cordari too. And that would have made things much easier for the murderer.'

'Not necessarily, sir. Small wiry chaps can be mighty tough.'

'I agree they can be, given the chance, but they're much easier to knock out unawares and to deal with afterwards.'

'It may be no more than a coincidence, sir. After all they were all of Mediterranean stock, and they go in for small men in that part of the world—like the Welsh, they are,' he added, as a pleased afterthought.

'Anyway, it's something to bear in mind,' Manton said.

'But if that pair of rubber boots we found here are anything to go by, sir, the murderer himself wasn't very large.'

'Yes, those boots!' Manton exclaimed. 'Though what you say doesn't necessarily follow. Some big people have quite small feet.'

'I can't see why they should have been left here at all. The whole place is as bare as Old Mother Hubbard's cupboard, apart from a pair of rubber boots sitting tidily on the floor. If he had time to clear away everything else that might incriminate him, why not the boots as well?'

'I don't know. Perhaps he knows that they won't or can't incriminate him. After all, it's less than an outside chance that we'll be able to trace them to a particular person. All they really do is purport to tell us the size of the murderer's feet.'

Talper gave vent to a long sigh and said gloomily:

'I've heard of someone being convicted by his cap, so, I suppose, why not his boots?'

Joe Mendolia returned to his flat shortly before noon. As he closed the front door behind him he suddenly halted in his tracks and sniffed. His face registered a series of quick-changing expressions. Doubt, surprise and hesitation were replaced by sardonic amusement and anticipation. He tiptoed across the lobby and flung open the door of the living-room.

'I smelt you outside,' he said with a grin as Pamela started up from the sofa. 'And you haven't even given yourself a drink. What's it to be—the usual?'

She shook her head.

'Not now, Joe. I want to talk to you.'

'Fine, but let's drink as well.'

'No, please.'

He gave a good-natured shrug.

'O.K., but I'm going to, even if you won't.' He walked over to a walnut cocktail cabinet in the corner of the room and poured himself a Scotch. 'Sorry; but now you'll have to wait while I fetch some ice,' he said, after peering around and failing to find any. He left the room and on return came and sat down beside her on the sofa. 'And now let me just light a cigarette and my ears are all yours.'

Pamela watched him seriously all this time. When he indicated that he was ready to listen, she said:

'Do you know anything about these men who've disappeared on bail from West End Court?'

If he was taken aback by the suddenness of her question, he did not manifest it by so much as the flicker of an eyelash.

'Ah! And what sort of thing do you expect me to know about them?' he asked.

'Joe, I want an answer. This is important to me.'

'I've guessed that, honey.'

'Well?'

'I've heard that they've probably been murdered and that one of them was a copper.'

'He was my brother-in-law.'

'Your brother-in-law?' This time there was genuine surprise in his tone. 'You had a brother-in-law who was a policeman?'

'He was in the Special Branch at the Yard.'

'I see,' he said slowly. 'Well, that's bad luck, isn't it? What can I do to help, honey? Is your sister O.K. for cash?'

Pamela bit her lip and seemed to find difficulty in speaking.

'Joe, there're rumours connecting you with what's happened.'

'You don't believe I go in for murder, do you? I mayn't keep all the ten Commandments, but I'm O.K. on that one. Anyway, why should I have killed these men?'

'Somebody has—and has made quite a lot of money out of it,' she said, watching him from beneath drooped lids.

'Oh, I see! Any law-breaking that makes a profit is credited to me, is that it?' He gave a short laugh. 'Well, murder's not my line of business at all. I can tell you that straight.'

'I wish I could believe that.'

'You will if you try hard enough,' he said cheerfully. 'Now you're going to have a drink.' He walked over to the cocktail cabinet and selected a half-bottle of champagne. 'All for you. You'll be on top of the world again in no time. Too bad about your brother-in-law, but this'll put you right.'

'Joe,' she said carefully, battling against odds which she felt were too great for her. 'Even though you don't know anything,

99

surely with all your contacts you could find something out quite easily.'

'Find out who runs this Soho branch of Murder Incorporated? Of course I'll keep my ears open if that's what you want, honey.'

'But, Joe——'

'That's enough of these "But, Joes". You drink this down and we'll go out and have a spot of lunch.'

She accepted the glass of champagne and looked at him helplessly as he clinked his own against it. She had completely failed to penetrate his armour and he had warded off her questions as though they'd been no more troublesome than soap bubbles. She sipped at her glass and determined to make one more effort.

'Are you *sure* you don't know something already?' she asked in an urgent tone.

'No more than you do, apparently. But I've promised I'll keep an ear to the ground and maybe I'll be able to let you know something later.' He put out a finger and lifted her chin. 'Now come on and drink up, honey.'

Their eyes met. Hers imploring, his shining but inscrutable.

When the court adjourned for lunch, Lord Droxford went straight to his room and retrieved from beneath the leather blotter on his desk the letter he'd received that morning from Algeria.

Reading it through for the second time, he decided that its contents were no better than he recalled from a first cursory glance. Carefully selecting a sheet of stamped notepaper from the tooled leather stationery box which adorned his desk, he started to write. He did so without pause or hesitation, and with the final flourish of his signature immediately folded the letter and sealed the envelope. After affixing the stamps, he placed it in an inside pocket of his jacket. Normally he left letters on the side of the desk for Plowman to collect and post, but not on this occasion.

Patting his pocket and being apparently satisfied that nothing further remained to be done, he rose and fetched his bowler hat and umbrella from the cupboard in the corner which they shared with a bag of golf clubs.

He was about to leave his room when the door suddenly opened and Mr. Astbury came in.

'Oh, I'm so sorry, sir,' he said, in obvious surprise at finding anyone there. 'I thought you'd gone to lunch.'

'I had something to attend to first. I'm just off now. Something you want?'

Mr. Astbury's features broke into a sheepish grin.

'I looked in to see if I could borrow your *Times*, sir.'

'It's over there on the desk.' As his eye fell on it, so he also noticed Heath's letter still lying half open beside it. He stepped forward and picked up both, handing the newspaper to Mr. Astbury and crumpling up the letter before stuffing it in his pocket.

'Many thanks, sir. I'll put it back on your desk later.' Mr. Astbury turned and left the room, followed a moment later by Lord Droxford.

Outside on the pavement, Lord Droxford acknowledged a constable's salute, glanced at his watch and set off for his club with a brisk, military stride. He invariably lunched at the Combined Universities Club, of which he was one of the more prominent members, and normally did so in relative leisure. But today was going to be a rush.

At the first letter-box he came to, he halted and, with a deliberation that marked all his acts, posted the letter he'd just written. He waited to hear it drop before continuing on his way.

On arrival at his club, the first thing he did was to tear Heath's letter into small pieces and consign them to anonymity in a waste-paper basket. Then he was ready for lunch.

Meanwhile, back at West End Court, Plowman and P.C. Tredgold were having theirs in the jailer's office, which for a few rare and precious minutes was empty and silent.

Tredgold had removed his jacket, and sitting with elbows propped on bulging blue thighs was munching a large sandwich. Near him, Plowman was inexpertly decanting coffee from a flask into a small plastic cup, much of the liquid dribbling on to the floor between his legs.

'Don't know why you trouble to bring that when you can always get a cup of tea here,' Tredgold said after watching him for a time.

'I prefer coffee.'

'No reason why you shouldn't make that here, too.'

'I dare say not, but I've got used to bringing it with me.'

'My wife won't make coffee. Says it's bad for the heart.'

'I make this myself. Wife has nothing to do with it.'

'How is she?'

'All right last time I saw her,' Plowman replied laconically.

'Left you then, has she?'

'Not exactly. She lives downstairs and I live up. We only meet occasionally.'

'That's no life.'

'It won't last for ever.'

Tredgold shot his companion a searching look.

'Got something in mind?'

'Could be.' The usher lowered his head and noisily sucked up some coffee.

'Well, don't go and knock her off and bury her body in the coal-hole,' Tredgold advised cheerfully.

Plowman chuckled.

'No; but I can well understand how some of these chaps are driven to doing such things.'

'Stupid and unsubtle lot, for the most part,' Tredgold remarked. 'Half the chaps who pass through here had no need to get caught if they'd used their loaves. A little forethought and the odds are they'd have got away with their misdeeds. Mind you, it's a good job they didn't; but they do seem to make it unnecessarily easy for the police sometimes.'

'From what I've heard this morning, this Sirena Street killer doesn't come into that category. He hasn't left many clues around.'

Tredgold pulled out his pipe and filled it in thoughtful silence.

'I've a feeling we're going to hear a lot more about that matter soon,' he said slowly.

'An early arrest, do you mean?'

'That seems to be about the last thing that'll happen. But my guess is that we'll soon have Manton and his aides round here like bees round a jam-pot.'

'He was here this morning.'

'I know he was. But that was just a preliminary look. You mark my words, Arnold, we're going to be turned upside down *and* inside out in the next few days. I'm pretty sure they think a clue to the case lies hidden right here at court.'

'What sort of clue?' Plowman asked with interest.

But Tredgold either didn't know or didn't wish to say, for he merely shook his head in a non-committal fashion.

The vaulted glass roof of the jailer's office at West End Court meant that on hot days the place became oven-like. Today was one such, and both men, being of heavy build, were glistening with perspiration.

Plowman took out a handkerchief and mopped his face all over.

'Shouldn't have drunk that coffee,' Tredgold opined.

'Hot drinks make you cooler. It's a well-known fact.'

'A well-know mother's tale. Just look at you, then. It stands to reason, Arnold, that you're heating up the blood drinking that stuff.'

Plowman bridled at this flat contradiction of one of his cherished beliefs.

'It doesn't go anywhere near the blood-stream.' He managed a chuckle at the idea of anything so ridiculous. 'Why, you're probably one of those people who believes that eating biscuits dries up the blood.' There was nothing like a counter-attack for restoring morale.

'Salt tablets are the thing in really hot weather.' Tredgold threw out this gratuitous and seemingly irrelevant piece of information with an air of complacency as he watched the usher mop round the inside of his collar. 'However, *we're* still a couple of fit 'uns, eh?' he added heartily.

'We certainly are, Albert. I reckon we could knock spots off any of the other courts in physical fitness.'

'And you couldn't find a happier court than ours either.'

Thus comfortably delivered, each turned once more to his food.

After leaving the tax office, Swift cut his way across town to Sirena Street. On the way he passed the telephone kiosk where Cordari had received his last fateful call. A young girl now occupied it, blithely unaware that it had so recently lured a man to his death. Farther on, he walked past Mustapha's shop above which Cordari had lodged, and a short distance beyond that a café where they used to meet and exchange news. Indeed, this whole area of Soho brought back a succession of memories of his friend; for though he had got to know Cordari only recently, there had developed between them in that short space of time a bond of friendship which had been fostered and fortified by the very nature of their assignment.

Swift gritted his teeth and strode on.

When he arrived at the shelter, he learnt that Manton had

been there and left again. The crowds had also thinned and, apart from a few merry-eyed urchins and a placid constable whom they were taunting from a safe distance, Sirena Street was enjoying its usual midday quiet.

'The old black girl at home?' Swift asked the constable who stood guard outside No. 28.

'She came back about ten minutes ago. How're things going?'

'As far as I'm concerned, hot and slowly,' Swift replied, tilting his hat to the back of his head and blowing out his cheeks. About the only thing he really objected to in his job was this having to wear a hat. There was no written rule about it, but it was one of the accepted conventions which a junior officer at the Yard flouted at his peril. Swift's hat was a rather dark green one, which he was able to wear at a wide variety of jaunty angles, according to his mood. 'I think I'll go in and see her.' He passed through the open door into the hall.

'It's the police,' he called out, knocking hard on the door of her room. 'Detective Constable Swift.' He heard her moving about inside and then the door opened an inch and her face appeared at the crack.

'You the one who was here last night with the other?'

'That's right. O.K. for me to come in?'

She grunted a reply and walked away, as though leaving him to please himself what to do.

He followed her and closed the door behind him. By this time she was seated in her chair beside the gas-ring, on which a kettle was boiling.

'Have you ever heard of a Mr. da Suva?' he asked. Though she was obviously aware of his presence in the room, her head went up in a gesture of testy surprise.

'You ask too many questions,' she growled.

'And you'll land yourself in trouble if you don't answer them.'

With his reply, she turned away and put out an unerring hand for the kettle which had started to hiss petulantly. He watched her brew a cup of coffee, fascinated by the instinctive movements she exhibited. Not once was there a moment of hazard or danger.

The room was fetidly hot, and partially drawn thick curtains shut out most of the light. Swift didn't think he'd be able to stay in there long.

'Who's da Suva?' he repeated.

Susannah shook her head impatiently.

'I know you've heard of him. He lives here, doesn't he?'

'No, I've already told you the names of the people who live here.'

'He owns the house, doesn't he?'

'I don't know,' she said, with the stubbornness of a child driven back on its last defence.

'But you know the name?' Swift pressed.

'I am a poor old black woman. Why do you want to worry me so? I can't help you any more, and yet you go on bullying me with questions. Perhaps you want to ruin me. Drive me away from my livelihood. But why, why? I've always lived honestly. Lord Droxford and Mr. Astbury know that.'

'All right, don't overdo the self-pity,' he broke in. 'All I'm asking you is a simple question.' At this point, he fished out his wallet and fingered a pound note so that Susannah could hear. 'Even the police can be generous sometimes—when people help them.' There followed a short silence. 'Now, who is da Suva?'

'Letters come for him here sometimes.'

Swift nodded with satisfaction.

'What happens to them?'

'The man who collects the rent takes them.'

'Is *he* Mr. da Suva?'

'No.'

'How do you know?'

'He says Mr. da Suva lives a long way off.'

'But has he told you who Mr. da Suva is?'

'Mr. da Suva is someone else.'

'You're not really dumb, so stop acting that way,' he said sternly.

'He is someone else, but I tell you I don't know who he is,' she replied, flaring up at his tone. 'If you know everything so much better than I do, why ask all your questions?'

'All right, calm down again. But how do you know who the letters are addressed to that arrive here?'

'Shirley—she's the girl on the top floor—brings them to me.'

'And you keep Mr. da Suva's until the rent man calls, is that it?' She nodded. Swift was silent and then suddenly asked: 'When is he due to call again?'

Susannah appeared to do a mental calculation. 'On Thursday,' she said flatly.

'What time?'

105

'In the evening.'

'Fine.' With a sudden dawning of suspicion he added: 'No trying to warn him off on your squeeze-box. If I hear you playing "The Desert Song" or anything like that tomorrow, you'll be in real trouble, old girl.'

She stared impassively in his direction, her sightless gaze directed at the wallet he still held in his hand.

He extracted a note and was about to hand it to her when he appeared to remember something Putting it away again, he fumbled deeper and suddenly produced the dispirited-looking one-pound note that Heath had given him and which he'd subsequently tucked right at the back of his wallet and forgotten about.

'Well, here you are. I doubt whether you've earned it, but perhaps you will.'

The old Negress's hand darted out to take it. Swift had folded the note once longwise and she now proceeded to open it out for the digital examination she gave all paper money. Watching her, he became aware that something untoward had happened. She muttered fiercely to herself and kept turning the note over as her fingers raced round its edges and over its surface.

'There's nothing wrong with it,' Swift said at last. 'It's only been a bit torn.'

'I recognize it. I've had it before. It was given me . . .' Once more the tips of her fingers swarmed across it.

'Yes, who by?' he asked excitedly.

'By someone outside the court one day.'

'Do you know who?' She shook her head. 'How long ago?'

'Several weeks.'

'Here, give it back,' he said, whisking it from her grasp. 'Have this one instead. It's new.'

Back at the Yard, Swift found Manton in his room, poring over a pile of papers.

Quickly he told him the results of his morning's inquiries, finishing up with his visit to Susannah. As he spoke, he pulled the note from his pocket and held it out for Manton to see.

'You say Heath gave you this in Algeria?'

'Yes, sir,' Swift replied, puzzled by Manton's tone and even more by the gesture that followed as he closed his eyes, screwed up his face and clapped a hand to his forehead.

A moment later, with a sudden flash of recollection, Manton said:

'I've seen it too. I remember now. It was at West End Court; it was part of the change given Mendolia when he was paying a fine there a few weeks back. It was the day Brufa failed to answer to his bail. The day this all started.'

'Then it must have been Mendolia who gave it to Susannah,' Swift said excitedly.

'What's really important is what she did with it afterwards?' He looked at Swift, whose jaw dropped stupidly.

'Great heavens! I completely forgot to ask her that. God, I'm an idiot! I was so carried away with the excitement of hearing she recognized it I——'

'Better get back there, quickly, now. Take a car.'

Swift arrived back at 28 Sirena Street just as Susannah was emerging from her room, her accordion swung over one powerful shoulder.

'A further question about that pound note?' he said breathlessly. 'Who did you give it to? I must know.'

For a moment there was silence, while she seemed to be taking stock of his sudden reappearance. Then brushing past him to go out and with an impatient hoist of her shoulder she said: 'I give it to the rent man.'

Swift's hands dropped to his side as he let her pass and watched her set off down the street in the direction of the court. He felt he might have known what her answer would be. Invariably everything now came back to the mysterious person of the rent collector, who had begun to loom over the investigation like a giant question mark.

CHAPTER SIXTEEN

As he journeyed out to Wimbledon that evening to see Pamela, Swift realized, perhaps for the first time, the extent to which the case was making inroads on his reserves of nervous energy, and how much he had come to rely on Pamela to replenish those reserves with her qualities of astringency and clear perspective. But first he had another call to make.

Pamela had, he knew, seen Doreen and broken to her the

news about Roy, Consequently he conceived it his duty to call on her himself, small relish though he had for such a visit in the circumstances. Indeed, as he directed his footsteps towards the Cordari home he anxiously rehearsed what he should say. What could one say that didn't sound trite and conventional?

He was still wrestling with his thoughts when he opened the garden gate and advanced up the short, red-tiled path towards the front door. Behind him, the gate closed with a click and he saw Doreen look up sharply from her chair in the front living-room.

'Hello, Kevin, won't you come in?' she said, opening the door as he reached there.

'Thanks.' He walked past her into the hall. From a covert glance, she looked pale but composed.

Juliet, who was sitting on the living-room floor as he entered, gave him a seraphic smile and waved a well-gnawed rusk. He smiled at her nervously.

'I was just about to take her upstairs to bed. I'm afraid she's rather late tonight,' Doreen said, stooping down to gather scattered oddments from around her small daughter.

'Would you like me to go then?' Swift asked awkwardly, still groping how to begin.

'Oh, no, please stay a bit. A few minutes won't make any difference.'

'Well, it mustn't be more than that. But I felt I had to come and tell you how ... terribly sorry I am about Roy.' Sincerity robbed the words of any mundaneness.

'I suppose ...' Her voice faltered. 'I suppose there's no question of a mistake? That perhaps it's not Roy after all?'

'I wish there was ...'

'Nobody's told me anything officially yet, I mean. Unless that's why you're here?'

'No; but I'm afraid there isn't much doubt about Roy being dead.'

'I see.' She blinked her eyes, and Swift could see the tears welling up, but her voice was under firm control as she went on speaking. 'Perhaps I'm only being knowledgeable after the event, and yet several times in the last two or three weeks I've had a premonition about this. Perhaps policemen's wives always have them; the same way that soldiers' wives often do in wartime.'

'If there's anything I can do, Doreen?'

She shook her head. 'Thank you all the same, Kevin.'

'I promise you that nobody's going to rest till we've tracked down who did it.' His tone sounded, to himself, falsely vehement and he blushed with embarrassment.

She nodded vaguely, as though not really listening to what he said.

He looked around the neatly furnished room, which, if in no way remarkable, was essentially part of a home—a home until recently of a small, devoted family. But one member of it had now gone for ever, leaving the other two to an uncertain future. Swift suddenly saw it all in brutal clarity: the pitiful pension which would never begin to cover the weekly outgoings; the job which would have to be taken and which would mean an inevitable separation from Juliet; the move to a furnished room which could never be home. His thoughts were interrupted by Juliet herself, who started to grizzle.

'She must be tired,' he said, jumping to his feet.

Doreen made no attempt to keep him. 'Thank you for looking in, Kevin. Some time when I've got straight, I'd like you to come in for supper one evening and we'll have a long talk . . . about Roy.'

When he reached the gate, he looked round and waved. Juliet waved back at him—over her mother's shoulder as Doreen turned to fasten the door against the outside world.

If anything had been needed to strengthen Swift's resolve, this last glimpse of Doreen Cordari and her baby would have provided it.

For this had ceased to be just another murder case (there was little that was 'ordinary' about it by any standards), and had now become a matter of sacred trust, of a pledge to find the murderer of Roy Cordari. If it had still been an age of taking formal avenging oaths, Kevin Swift and Pamela would have sworn theirs.

As Swift turned into the quiet, ill-lit road where Pamela lived, his mood lightened and he quickened his pace. Her flat lay on the top floor of a solid semi-detached Victorian structure, of a type which has multiplied itself in all the older London suburbs. Long before he reached the house, he saw the light shining from her living-room.

Tired though he was, he bounded up the stairs with a light step. The front door of the flat was ajar and he entered, closing it behind him and dropping the catch.

'I'm in here,' she called out from the living-room. Swift smiled to himself in hopeful anticipation, adjusted his tie and went in.

She was sitting on the couch with her legs up and a magazine in her lap. He came straight across and kissed her once, and then immediately a second time rather more ardently.

'That one's to make up for my not having been able to when we met this morning.'

'It's obviously been accumulating interest during the day,' she replied, pushing him gently away from her. 'You smell very fresh.'

'I had a shower and shave just before coming out.'

'Oh!' she said, and looked at him quizzically.

Swift smirked, rather than smiled, at her. Despite the strain of recent events, he appeared full of eagerness. It was a quality which Pamela found agreeable. She also liked his funny cropped hair, his very small, very white teeth and his wide, mobile mouth. She turned away, determined not to succumb to the erotic thoughts which, she freely acknowledged to herself, were often evoked with dangerous ease.

'Was Mendolia very cross when you broke your date with him for tonight?' Swift asked.

'Not really,' she replied casually.

'Do you think he knows anything about the case?'

'I told you on the 'phone what he said.'

'M'mm, it rather seems he's got us dangling on the end of a string over that now. I mean, if he's in things up to his neck, he'll just feed you spurious bits of information to keep you quiet. And if he's not, well . . . he'll probably do the same anyhow.'

'You don't seem to have much faith in his promise to help get at the truth of Roy's death.'

'Have *you*, then?' Swift's tone was scornful, and Pamela made no reply. He failed to notice the worried look deep down in her eyes. 'Our hope is that you'll be able to pick up something apart from what he *wants* you to know. Frankly, I'm not sure it was very wise to tell him that Roy was your brother-in-law. If he believes you're working for the police, he'll certainly throw out all the false leads he can.' He paused and frowned, 'Moreover, you might be in some personal danger. And if there's any chance of that, you're not to spend a second more in his company. You promise me that, don't you?' His voice was suddenly vibrant with emotion. 'I could never live if I knew I'd been responsible for any harm coming to you.'

She put out a hand and rested it lightly on his sleeve. 'You're very sweet, Kevin; but I'll be all right. It's you I'm worried about.' She gazed at him with the wistful expression of a mother who knows rather better than her child the tribulations that lie ahead. She half expected him to repudiate her solicitude with male heartiness. But instead he said quietly:

'I'm glad.'

'I went to see Doreen this evening,' she went on quickly. 'She's being terribly brave about Roy. It's funny, isn't it, the way people you think you know really well suddenly reveal unexpected traits? She's exhibiting an almost fatalistic streak which I never knew she possessed. I offered to stop with her, but she wouldn't hear of it.'

Swift described his own visit to Doreen Cordari, and for some while after this their conversation was of life and how it ought to be lived. It was a serious exchange, only dissolving into occasional flippancies when either felt the danger of revealing those deep inner thoughts reference to which is so un-British.

In due course they got back to the case and its prospects of solution.

'Mr. Manton's a fine officer,' he remarked loyally. 'He'll not leave anything undone. And as far as I'm concerned, the case'll never be written off unsolved. Whatever happens I'll get to the truth, even if it takes me the rest of my life working single-handed. Though that's not likely to be necessary.' His expression relaxed. 'Are you seeing Mendolia tomorrow?'

'He's going to 'phone me.'

'I wonder what he really knows? He's mixed up in so much ... I shouldn't be surprised if Mr. Manton didn't decide to haul him in for questioning.'

Pamela looked at him sharply.

'Do you think that's possible?'

He shrugged his shoulders in an expression of indifference. How could he tell? It would probably depend on what happened in the next twenty-four hours. His thoughts turned elsewhere, to matters of more immediate interest. He looked at his watch and simulated startled surprise.

'Good heavens, it's after one,' he said.

Pamela eyed him benignly. 'That means you've missed the last bus and tube back into Town.'

111

'I'm afraid I have.'

'You'd better stop here for the night.'

'Is that O.K.?'

'Sure,' she said, jumping up to leave the room. 'I'll fetch you a couple of blankets. You'll find the couch quite comfortable. And the end lets down so you can stick your feet out.'

Swift's expression of eager anticipation slowly dropped from his face to be replaced by a sickly smile. He caught sudden sight of this in a wall mirror and crossly removed it.

After Pamela had brought him the blankets, wished him a friendly good night and firmly closed the door as she went out, he ruefully gazed at himself in the mirror and kicked off his shoes. It was going to be a somewhat different night from the one he'd hopefully looked forward to.

Despite the alleged charms of the couch, he awoke next morning with a stiff neck and with pins and needles in his right leg, which felt as though it had become detached from his body. Pulling a blanket over his head, he turned on his other side and dozed off again into a disgruntled sleep.

The next thing he knew was that the blanket had been whisked off him and a cool hand was tousling his hair. He opened an eye and saw Pamela, fully dressed, regarding him with amusement.

'Poor Kevin,' she said, and suddenly bent down and lightly kissed him on the cheek. 'You'd better go and have a shave. You're bristly.'

'No razor.'

'You'll find one in the bathroom. I'll get breakfast, so don't linger.'

Sure enough, in the bathroom he found a tube of brushless cream and a safety razor, laid out ready for him.

'How come you keep a razor in this maiden's apartment?' he called out to her in the kitchen as he smeared his face with the cream.

'Somebody left it here. A long time ago,' she added but declined to be drawn further on the subject.

Breakfast consisted of coffee, cereal, bacon omelette and lots of toast and marmalade.

'Not bad,' Swift said as he surveyed the tray she bore in.

'Don't think I have all this when I'm alone. In fact I'm not having it now. Two cups of unsugared coffee and one slice of unbuttered toast is all my waistline allows me to eat.'

'Trying to get my sympathy?'

'Hardly.' And with a malicious gleam in her eye, she added:
'Any more than you could expect to get mine.'

Big Ben was striking half past eight when Swift emerged
from the Westminster Underground station and turned on to
the Embankment. Two minutes later he was in the office he
shared with five other detective constables. For the moment he
had it to himself and it presented an unusual scene. Normally
half its occupants were trying to make telephone calls, while the
other half were interviewing people or dictating reports. The
resultant bedlam was stunning to anyone not used to it.

Swift walked across to the desk in the far corner which was
his. It was extravagantly untidy and littered with half-completed reports, statements and a multitude of other documents.
All seemed very remote and unimportant compared with the
matter in hand. He idly picked up a report he'd been trying to
get finished on the activities of a triple bigamist. Heaven knew
when he'd be able to pick up the threads of that again. And,
anyway, what did it matter? The man in question was an un-
obtrusively cheerful character who was now happily settled with
a newly acquired wife who bore him no ill will for his deceit.
Indeed, it had been a remarkable feature that none of his wives
appeared to bear him any grudge at all. They'd all enjoyed his
company while it lasted and later accepted philosophically his
quixotic change of partner. Whether he would eventually be
labelled a monster and be sent to prison for some years, or
whether he would leave the court a free man with a few judicial
cynicisms ringing in his ears, would depend entirely on the per-
sonality of the people who tried him. Such was life, capricious
and chancy, and seldom, so far as the law was concerned, the
desiccated calculating machine that people so fondly imagined.

The bell on Swift's 'phone extension suddenly rang and he
lifted the receiver.

'D.C. Swift here.'

'This is Superintendent Manton. Come along to my room
right away, will you?'

'Yes, sir.' Swift replaced the receiver with a gasp. What could
he want at this hour of the morning? Admittedly a quarter to
nine wasn't all that early, but Swift was nevertheless surprised.

He hurried along to Manton's office. The Superintendent was
standing by his desk, hat in hand, when he entered.

'We're going to St. Michael's Hospital to see Dr. Anselm,' he said briskly. 'He promised he'd let me have a preliminary report this morning.'

They made their way downstairs and to a waiting car.

'St. Michael's Hospital,' Manton said to the driver as they both got into the back.

As they drove slowly under the archway which spanned the two limbs of the building, Swift threw a grin at one of his room-mates who was just arriving. Since he'd been assigned to his present job, he'd scarcely seen anything of his own colleagues, but knew that he was the object of their envy. It was rarely given to a humble D.C. to work quite so closely with a detective superintendent on a major inquiry.

The car turned on to the Embankment and headed East. St. Michael's, one of the large London hospitals, was where Dr. Anselm had the use of a laboratory and of a staff of enthusiastic assistants.

'If he's able to identify the remains of any one body, we're O.K.,' Manton said. 'Otherwise it's going to be one heck of a problem persuading a court that anyone's been murdered.'

Swift pondered this for a moment. It seemed to him that the problem of catching the murderer was by far the more formidable. Once that was accomplished, it wasn't essential to produce bits of body as evidence of murder. He could recall two cases in recent years where no body had ever been found and in each the accused had yet been convicted. With slight diffidence he mentioned this to Manton.

'Yes, but don't you see, in each of those two cases, there was strong evidence connecting the accused with a person who had vanished in suspicious circumstances and whose sudden death could be inferred from a wealth of circumstantial detail.'

'That could still happen in this case, sir.'

'Yes; but on the other hand we may be hard put to it to connect a suspect, once we have one, with any of the men who've disappeared and, as we believe, been murdered, unless we're able to prove that any of them ever went near the shelter. Positive identification of a single one of them will be sufficient to bridge that gap.'

For the remainder of the journey they continued to discuss evidential aspects of the case. They reached the hospital, a huge straggling building, or rather series of buildings, and pulled up outside a door above which there appeared the faded legend

'Department of Pathology'. Manton led the way in.

He knew the geography of the place almost as well as that of the Yard, and made straight for an office half-way down a long corridor which smelt strongly of formaldehyde and floor polish. The door was open, but there was no one inside. At that moment a white coated figure came through the swing doors at the end of the corridor.

'Is Dr. Anselm in the lab.?' Manton asked.

'Yes. Do you want him?'

'Don't bother. I know my way in.'

Swift followed Manton through the swing doors which led to the laboratory. Inside, all the smells that abounded without were multiplied. Two tousle-headed young men and an Indian girl were grouped round a complicated structure of tubes and retorts. Beyond them, Dr. Anselm was bending over one of the tables with his back to them.

It reminded Swift very much of glorious hours spent in the school laboratory, successfully bedevilling the chemistry master's experiments.

'May we come in?' Manton asked, somewhat superfluously, as he walked over to where Dr. Anselm was at work.

At first sight it looked as though the doctor was studying a row of museum fossils, which were laid out on the table in front of him.

He looked up.

'Hello, Manton. So far we've salvaged this lot from the sludge; though I doubt whether there's anything more to come.'

'Look like bits of bone, sir,' Swift said eagerly.

'That's just what they are. Small fragments of human bone which the acid never dissolved.'

'Definitely human?' Manton put in.

'Quite definitely. My anatomy's a bit rusty, so I got that bunch of young blood over there,' he nodded in the direction of the trio—'who've passed exams in the subject far more recently than I have, to see what they could identify.' He picked up a short thin splinter that looked as if it might have come from a hen. 'This is one of the bones that run down the back of the hand.' He seized Swift's right hand and demonstrated. 'And this one'—he picked up another bit—'is part of a shin-bone. And this next to it, which has been pretty badly attacked by the acid, is a lump of thigh-bone.'

'But is there anything which helps to identify a particular

person?' Manton asked, as his eyes took in the line of assembled exhibits.

Dr. Anselm gazed at him with a faintly reproachful expression.

'Isn't it enough for the moment to be told that these are human remains, and no doubt about it?' he asked in a pained tone.

'Yes, of course, Doctor, but we had more or less gathered that from the scene itself.'

'And now I'm telling you it's a certainty. Not only from these pieces of bone, but also from small deposits of human fat we recovered from the wall of the drain and from that oil drum.'

He lifted his gaze to the corner of the laboratory where the drum incongruously rested. 'By the way, it's tar-lined, you know.'

Manton followed the digression. 'Would that have protected it against the acid?'

'Certainly.'

'It must have required an awful lot of acid each time, sir,' Swift said. 'It's almost the size of a rain-water butt and with a body in it that had to be covered . . .'

'He wouldn't have used neat acid—not commercial sulphuric acid, that is. He'd have diluted it. Far more effective. Haigh discovered that.'

'While we're on this subject, how long do you reckon it took him to dissolve a body?' Manton asked.

Dr. Anselm screwed up his face in thought. 'Would depend on size, etcetera; but about a week, I should say. To do the job properly, that is.'

Manton now returned his attention to the pieces of bone. 'It's all very well knowing these are human remains, but we've got to go farther. We've got to establish who the victims were. Incidentally, does one assume that these pieces have all come from the same person?'

'Further tests'll be required for that, and they'll take time. We shall have to examine the bone structure and composition in each case to discover whether they could have, might have, or quite definitely have not come from the same body.'

'Are there no other bits you've recovered?' Manton asked, letting his gaze roam hopefully around the laboratory.

Dr. Anselm appeared to study him with sardonic amusement.

'One tooth,' he said slowly.

'A tooth? But that's terribly important. We may be able to identify someone by it.'

'Indeed, yes, and I hope we shall. It's a single artificial tooth made of some plastic material.'

'Part of a set of dentures?'

'No. What's called a crown. Fits into the original tooth socket. They're usually found where a single tooth has been lost. Knocked out for example, playing some game or other.'

'Where is the tooth?'

'Can you bring it over here a moment, Bailey?' Dr. Anselm called out to one of his assistants. It arrived in a small cylindrical container where it nestled on cotton wool like a precious stone.

Manton and Swift gazed at it with rapt expressions.

'Presumably all these pieces of body are more likely to come from one of the later, as opposed to the earlier, victims?'

'The odds are in favour of their being from the last of all. That's your chap, isn't it?'

Manton nodded. 'We can easily get hold of Cordari's dental record card.'

'I put through a call shortly before you arrived and they were going to call me back.'

'We'll chase them up again.' Manton looked round for a telephone. 'Did you know anything about his having a false tooth?' he asked Swift, as he made his way over to one in the far corner of the laboratory.

'No, sir.' Swift tried to remember what Cordari's teeth had looked like when he opened his mouth. From the fact that he could recall nothing, he assumed they were neither very good nor very bad. Roy had certainly never mentioned having a false one; but then it was not the sort of thing one made a point of talking about. Maybe he was rather sensitive about it. People were sometimes, as much about their teeth as about a boil on the behind.

While these thoughts were passing through his mind, Manton was making his phone call.

When he rejoined them, he said in a flat, expressionless tone:

'That seems to be Cordari's tooth all right.'

CHAPTER SEVENTEEN

A few hours later it was indisputably established that the tooth was Cordari's. It transpired that he had lost its predecessor, playing cricket a few years before, and been fitted with the one whose timely survival might now mean all the difference between a case solved and unsolved.

In the succeeding two days, there were no further developments and the whole inquiry settled down into a routine of painstaking thoroughness that marks most criminal investigations.

Door-to-door visits by various officers were made in Sirena and Syracuse Streets, and dozens of statements were taken. Most of them were negative and totally unhelpful. Manton himself interviewed anyone who was able to give any information at all, but none of it amounted to anything.

The manufacturers of the pair of rubber boots which had been found in the shelter were eventually traced, but were unable to say more than that between January and May they'd dispatched several thousand similar pairs to retailers all over the country, and had no possible means of identifying the pair in question.

A day-and-night watch was kept on 28 Sirena Street, in the course of which several of top-floor Shirley's gentlemen clients found themselves taken off for questioning, to their surprise and dismay and Shirley's vituperative indignation.

For the moment, the Press were continuing to give the case extravagant coverage—though no one knew better than Manton how quickly their interest would dwindle without the spur of constant fresh developments; until at last it would be quietly dropped into cold obscurity, leaving the police to weeks and possibly months of unglamorous routine.

Together, he and Swift had interviewed all the relatives and friends of the supposed victims, studied every record of them that existed and finally quizzed everyone at West End Court who had had any contact with them.

This had led Manton to seek a private talk with Lord Droxford after the court had risen one evening. But the magistrate had been tight-lipped and unforthcoming, and particularly reluctant to answer any questions about the ex-usher, Heath.

'Let's just say I gave a lame dog a helping hand,' he had said with an expression of well-bred distaste.

'You got him his job as a clerk, I believe, on Monsieur de Varin's farm in Algeria?' Manton persisted gently.

'That's my brother-in-law's place. He happened to need someone at the time.'

'Have you had any contact with him since, sir? Heath I mean?'

Lord Droxford frowned. 'The occasional Christmas card. That's about all.'

And that, too, was about all Manton learnt from him. Furthermore, he had resolutely declined to be drawn into any speculation about the missing defendants, or on the coincidence of their all coming from his court.

Manton's interview with Mendolia consisted of a series of thrusts by the one and bland parries by the other. On the face of it he had less to impart than those at West End Court, and this was the standpoint from which he refused to be budged.

'It was you who got Heath the sack, wasn't it?' Manton asked him.

'If you say so.'

'Kept in touch with him since he left the country?'

'No. Any reason why I should have?'

'That's what I'd like to know.'

'Me, too. Let me know if you find out.'

Manton then tried a different tack. 'You own a good deal of property around Soho, don't you?'

'Not Number twenty-eight Sirena Street, if that's what you're thinking.'

'Any idea who does own it?'

'No. Haven't you been able to discover, then?'

Soon after this, Manton had terminated a somewhat unsatisfactory interview. He obviously wasn't going to get anything out of Mendolia, or anyone else for that matter, until he knew a good deal more himself. But how was he learn more without probing all the likely spots? It was a bit like drilling for oil. You went on puncturing the earth's crust until you struck the stuff. In a criminal investigation you went on asking questions until you got a likely lead.

Inevitably, he and Swift were pinning their foremost hopes on being able to identify the mysterious rent collector, who, according to Susannah, was due to call at 28 Sirena Street on Thursday evening.

119

As the day approached, it became more and more apparent that his entry on the scene was going to receive the full range of spotlights, and that if he missed his cue and failed to show up the police were likely to find themselves face to face with a high blank wall.

It was a bleak prospect. If the man was implicated in the murders, he wouldn't be likely to appear. If he did—then surely he must be innocent. Either way things looked far from hopeful. At best, Thursday could be viewed only as a very small hump on an otherwise flat landscape.

In the event, however, it proved to be a day both of enterprise and caprice.

Heath awoke that morning at six o'clock, as usual, though he had not fallen asleep until after four.

Shafts of bright sunlight filtered through the wooden shutters of his bedroom window. He got up and drifted into the small kitchen. There he splashed some cold water in his face and combed his hair, staring dispassionately at himself in the inadequate piece of mirror propped above the sink.

After that, he put the coffee on the stove and sat down to watch it. When it was really hot he poured it into a large thick mug and drank it slowly and thoughtfully. It was black and very strong, the way he'd grown to like it. He appreciated especially the speed with which it dissolved all lingering traces of sloth. Though today there were none of these, for he'd been as wide awake when he got out of bed as the moment before he'd been suddenly eclipsed by sleep less than two hours ago.

A shirt, a pair of shorts and some sandals and he was dressed. Stepping outside the small, white, cube-like structure that was his home, he gazed across the road which separated it from Monsieur de Varin's, across the falling ground to the shore and the ever-sparkling blue sea beyond. This was by far the loveliest period of the day. The sun, though hot, had not yet sucked up all the fragrance that night had restored to Mother Earth.

Already teams of Arabs were at work in the vineyards and among the orange groves. Heath could see them moving about the distant landscape. He looked at his watch. It was twenty past six, the hour at which he always set off for the farm office a quarter of a mile away, where, first thing each morning, he collated records of items dispatched for sale the day before.

Closing the door of his house behind him, he walked a few

120

yards along the road and then took the dirt track which branched off to the left and led to where he and Swift had conducted their meeting. When he reached the acacia tree beneath which they'd stood, he paused in its shade and sat down.

He felt strangely at peace with the world: a peace he hadn't known before. For so long now, life had been a grey and solitary existence. Indeed, he never could remember it having been anything approaching a state of joy or blessedness; but since his exile it had been without hope.

Even recognizing, as he did, that it was his own moral weakness that had defeated him in a succession of life's conflicts, habit inclined him still to place the major blame on those who had exploited him, as he chose to believe, for their own predatory ends.

But at last that was now finished with. There was going to be no more shadow-wrestling with a punch-drunk conscience.

A sudden upsurge of self-pity was but momentary and did little to ruffle the sense of peace that blanketed his mind. He was past nurturing personal animosities; past rehearsing useless recriminations.

As he sat beneath the tree watching an ox-cart laboriously move up the hillside, his thoughts leapt across the frontiers of sea and land and came to West End Court. In a few hours' time, they'd be reassembling there for another day's work. Lord Droxford, Mr. Astbury, Mr. Turnbull, and the rest. No longer, however, would any of them be able to impinge upon his weaknesses.

But what was he waiting for? For the first time in years he'd thought something out and reached a decision, albeit one heavily circumscribed by events. It had taken him the greater part of the night hours, but with the decision had finally come a pure, dreamless sleep. No more would he be a piece of driftwood carried into stagnant by-waters by the tide of stronger wills. He was filled with a hitherto unknown strength of purpose, which had brought him this miraculous release from anxiety. Let others now look after themselves, for he was about to elude their machinations for ever.

With an almost casual gesture, he drew out a revolver and shot himself cleanly through the head.

It was six o'clock that evening when news of Heath's suicide reached Manton. The report he received went on to add that a letter had been found on the dead man which might help to explain the affair. This was being forwarded to Scotland Yard immediately.

'Does his death surprise you?' Manton asked Swift, after passing the news on to him.

'Not really, sir,' Swift said in a slow, thoughtful tone. 'I won't pretend I was expecting it, but he was certainly the sort of chap for taking the easy way out.' Manton let the remark pass, though he himself often found it difficult to accept the popular conception of suicide being a coward's escape. Swift went on: 'I wonder if it was the result of someone putting pressure on him?'

'We'll know more about that when we see the letter. They might at least have told us who it was from.' Manton looked at his watch. 'It's time we got along to Sirena Street. Susannah said the man usually called for the rent between seven and eight.'

'Think he'll turn up, sir?'

'Frankly, no. And in one sense, I almost hope he doesn't, since that'll mean he's windy and daren't show himself.' Swift wasn't sure that he followed the logic of this, but refrained from saying so. 'If someone does turn up, the odds are he'll know nothing. It'll just be another link in the chain, making the darned thing a bit longer, but not necessarily bringing one any nearer its end.'

'It all seems rather like a game of snakes and ladders, sir. You plod along steadily, hoping all the time for throws which'll bring you nearer the solution but not infrequently collecting those that slide you back to the beginning again.'

'A pretty good analogy,' Manton said. 'I must remember it the next time I have to give a lecture to recruits. "... Criminal investigation is like a game of snakes and ladders ..." Yes, I like that.' He savoured the phrase approvingly.

To Swift, however, it had simultaneously occurred that almost every facet of living could be so likened if you put your imagination to it.

Sirena Street appeared to be empty of people when they arrived, though in fact No. 28 was being kept under observation, and had been, both day and night since the discovery in the shelter.

Manton and Swift entered, and Manton knocked on Susannah's door. 'Open up.'

There were the usual muttered grumbles from within and

then the old woman opened the door a crack. 'Has he been yet?' She shook her head impatiently. 'Or tried to get in touch with you at all?' Again there was a brusque gesture of denial. 'Have you got the money ready for him?' This time she closed her eyes as though weary of his questions and nodded. 'Let's see.' She ambled away from the door and the two men entered.

On the table was a purse which she snatched up and slithered out of sight under one of the folds of her outer clothing.

'I want to see the money,' Manton said firmly. 'I'm not going to steal it.'

The purse reappeared in her hand, and opening it she took out a bundle of notes. Manton counted them.

'Is this what you've collected from Shirley and Pepito and the others?'

'Don't you touch it. I'll be the one who gets into trouble if it's not all there.'

'Stop fretting: nobody's going to take any of it.'

'Give it me back.'

Manton did so. He turned to Swift.

'Right, I'll wait in here; you keep out of sight somewhere at the back of the hall.'

Swift left the room and took up a position near the kitchen where he'd be able to see them by moving his head very slightly.

The air around him was warm and smelt of stale cooking fat. In the stillness, he could hear, coming from a neighbouring house, the short mechanical bursts of febrile laughter that are seemingly designed to signpost the jokes in TV shows. From somewhere nearer came the sounds of a pair of shoes being dropped on a floor. Presumably one of Shirley's more fastidious customers.

He was beginning to think that Manton was going to be proved correct when he heard a light sound from the front of the hall. Someone had come in and had stopped near to Susannah's door. Almost immediately there were three soft knocks.

Cautiously Swift peeped round the angle of the wall.

A man stood in the doorway—unobtrusive and yet unsurreptitious; and quietly, wordlessly, held out his hand.

Innocent or guilty, the rent collector of 28 Sirena Street had come.

Arnold Plowman, the usher at West End Court!

CHAPTER EIGHTEEN

By the time the door opened and Plowman found himself face to face with Manton, Swift had moved silently forward to cut off the usher's retreat. But Plowman showed no signs of wanting to retreat; nor indeed, of any dismay at the sudden turn of events. He stood quietly waiting for Manton to speak.

'I'd like you to come to the Yard,' Manton said, raising his eyes in challenge to the usher's. But Plowman merely nodded in acquiescence and turned to follow Swift out to the waiting car. 'You, too, old girl. Come along!' Manton added, facing back into the room.

'Me! Where? What do you want with me?'

'You're going to take a short car ride to Scotland Yard. If you behave yourself, you won't be there long and we'll drive you home again.'

Susannah stared suspiciously about her. Then slowly she heaved herself up and, muttering darkly, put on her hat and coat. Manton waited patiently, and, when she was ready, took her by the elbow and steered her out to the car.

The journey to Scotland Yard was accomplished in oppressive silence. When they arrived, Manton and Plowman went ahead, leaving Swift to bring along the old Negress. More resentful than ever now, she refused to budge until he gave her his arm, though this merely provided her with a further opportunity of demonstrating her abrased feelings. Dragging on him heavily and making small angry noises, they made nightmare progress through the building. When at last they reached the corridor where Manton's office was, Manton stepped out and told Swift to put her in an djoining room and then come into his.

Plowman was sitting at ease when Swift entered. He looked politely interested in his surroundings and appeared completely relaxed.

'Got your notebook handy?' Manton said to Swift as he sat down. He turned back to Plowman. 'How long have you been collecting the rent from Twenty-eight Sirena Street?'

'Ever since I became usher at West End.'

'A couple of years?'

'About that.'

'Who's the owner of the property?'

Plowman looked nonplussed for a moment. He opened his mouth to speak but closed it without doing so. Then he said almost shyly: 'I don't know.'

'You must know who you pay the money to?'

'But I don't. I know it sounds absurd, and perhaps you'd like me to explain. Soon after I first went to work at West End, I received an anonymous letter asking me to act as a sort of agent for the writer in certain matters. I was given to understand that it was one of the regular sidelines for the usher at that court. You know, one of the perks of office. I gathered my predecessor had done it, too.'

'What did you get out of it?'

'Fifteen per cent of what I collected, to the nearest quid over.'

'How much did that amount to in a year?'

'About a hundred pounds.' With a wintry grin, he added: 'Tax free, of course.'

'If you never knew who you were acting for, how did you remit the money you'd collected?'

'Yes, I thought you'd ask that soon.' He frowned and plucked at a bristly hair on the tip of his nose. 'My instructions were always the same. To leave it in a sealed envelope behind a certain loose brick in a certain wall.' He took a deep breath and went on, with a rush: 'It's the wall on the blind side of West End Court. The one flanking that passage which runs up to a block of offices.' He looked at Manton as though for a cue and abruptly stopped.

'Yes, go on,' Manton urged.

'I always had to leave the money there as soon as I'd collected it. I used to take an envelope along with me to put it in . . .'

'I presume you deducted your commission first?' Manton remarked dryly.

'Yes, I made sure of that.' He paused. 'And at that hour of course, the offices at the end of the passage were all closed and there was never anyone about.'

'Didn't you ever stop to see who came for it?' Manton's blue eyes bored into the usher as he asked the question.

'No. I was warned not to hang about afterwards. And I didn't.' He seemed to feel that some further explanation was required. 'It's healthier to do as one's told when you're dealing with the boys who run Soho.'

'And what about paying the rates and taxes on the house?

Was that also arranged through you?'

'Yes. I used to receive the money for that in the same way. That is, it used to be left for me behind the brick.'

'Do you know the name in which the property is registered?'

'Da Suva,' Plowman said in a dispirited tone.

'Do you know Pepito, who owns the workshop in Syracuse Street?' Plowman nodded. 'How?'

'I've ordered stuff from him.'

'What stuff?'

Plowman wriggled uncomfortably.

'You know what. Acid.'

'Tell me about it,' Manton said in a quiet, steely voice.

'There's very little to tell, sir. I ordered it from time to time on instructions—anonymous instructions by post.'

'Got any of the written instructions still?'

'No.'

'What did you do with the acid when it came?'

'I didn't do anything with it. I told Pepito to leave it outside the door of that disused shelter. And I assume he always did. I never saw the stuff myself.'

A deep silence ensued in which Swift watched Plowman intently and Manton stared in a preoccupied way at his desk. When he looked up, he said:

'Was it on your instructions that Susannah used to include "The Desert Song" in her repertoire on certain days?'

'Yes, it was. That is, I passed her on the instructions I myself had received,' Plowman added wearily.

'Used you to listen for it when you were in court?'

'Yes, I suppose I did. I always wondered whom it was meant for?'

'Did you ever notice anyone in court showing particular interest in it or apparently waiting for it?'

'No. And I specially used to watch out for some reaction of that sort.'

'What precisely were the instructions you received?'

'I use to receive an anonymous typed note telling me to notify Susannah to be on the alert on a certain day and to play that particular piece if anyone dropped a threepenny bit and a halfpenny into her tin.'

'What was the postmark on all these notes you received?' Manton asked.

'Always London W.1.'

'And where were they sent you?'

Swift noticed that Plowman hesitated a second before answering, as though the question had caught him off balance.

'At court,' he said emphatically.

'Then others may have noticed them?'

'No, because I'm the person who sorts and distributes the mail.'

'And when you're away?'

'One of the juniors in Mr. Astbury's office. But as far as I know, none of these letters have been sent when I've been away. At least, I was never handed any when I got back.'

'Did you ever connect any of this with the defendants who vanished on bail from your court?'

'From time to time I've connected it with practically everything that was remotely suspicious and which happened within the court's jurisdiction.'

Manton sat back and studied the usher in long, silent appraisal. It was in many ways a fantastic story and yet not far different from what he might have expected. Hadn't he told Swift that if anyone turned up at Sirena Street, he'd probably be only a cog in the machine; another link man? The bosses in the crime world had always taken good care to insulate themselves against detection by employing tiers of middle-men who were paid well to do as they were told and not inquire where their orders came from. Someone had clearly seen the potential uses of West End Court's ushers and had put them on the payroll. Moreover, it appeared in the case of Heath, that he'd continued to be employed even after he left England. Gangsters' contracts with their employees mightn't be written; moreover there seldom had to be recourse to any enforcement clauses. When there was, however, it was sharp and effective.

Leaning forward again, Manton said in a quiet, even tone:

'You must have guessed the police would be waiting for you when you came along to Susannah's house this evening.' He paused, noting the alertness with which Plowman listened every time he opened his mouth. 'So why did you come?'

Plowman nodded as though to acknowledge the question's merit.

'Yes, I knew you'd be waiting. I—sort of wanted you to catch me. This thing's been preying on my mind. You've no idea what it's been like ever since you found what had been happening in the shelter.' He sighed heavily. 'That's the truth.'

127

There was an appreciable pause before anyone spoke again. Then Manton said:

'When was the last occasion your unknown employer made contact with you?'

'I haven't heard a word for several weeks. Not since your chap disappeared. Skourasi, wasn't it?'

'Have you any ideas about who's behind all this?'

'God knows! I've thought about it often enough. In my own mind, I'm convinced that Mendolia is the real Mr. Big.'

'You believe he's the person you've been working for all this time?' Manton asked bitingly. Plowman winced at the tone and dropped his head. Turning to Swift, Manton said: 'Bring in Susannah.' When she arrived, still protesting, in the room, Manton continued: 'I want to know whether you recognize someone's voice, so just listen carefully for a moment.' He motioned to Plowman to say something.

' 'Evening, Susannah, I've come for the rent money.'

The old Negress's head weaved suspiciously as the other three occupants of the room closely watched her.

'Yes, that's his voice,' she said sullenly.

During the following minutes, Manton vigorously cross-questioned the two of them. By the end, he had satisfied himself that there were no significant discrepancies in their respective stories. Certainly there was nothing in what Susannah had earlier told the police (and still adhered to) to give the lie to anything Plowman had said.

'O.K., we'll take you home now, old girl,' he said, getting up from the desk. 'Just before you go, Mr. Plowman, perhaps you wouldn't mind slipping off your shoes and letting Detective Constable Swift measure your feet.'

If the usher was surprised by the request, he didn't show it.

'They're uncommonly large,' he said, as Swift knelt and made pencil marks on a large, blank sheet of paper.

As he got up again, Swift gave Manton a quick shake of the head. It was clear that Plowman could never have worn the rubber boots found in the shelter.

Soon after Plowman and Susannah had left, Manton proposed an immediate visit to Mendolia's flat.

They left the building and Manton led the way towards his own private car which was parked in the yard. He took the Whitehall exit and drove up that broad thoroughfare towards

Trafalgar Square. It was just after midnight and the streets were relatively deserted. London, for all her size and world importance, was an early-to-bed old lady. And, anyway, those who hadn't yet gone home were not out on the streets. The English are not a night-strolling people like some, and understandably so in view of their climate.

Up Lower Regent Street, across Piccadilly Circus and then up Regent Street itself they drove. Swift stared vacantly out of the window at the narrow, dimly lit streets which ran off into the heart of Soho. Was the mystery of Cordari's death to be solved somewhere in there, he wondered. 'It's only when there's not much traffic about that you can see how hilly the West End is,' Manton said conversationally, as they turned left into Oxford Street, whose switchback contours were never more obvious.

When they reached Marble Arch, he continued west along Bayswater Road.

'It's one of these blocks on the right overlooking the park.'

'Yes, sir. The one just beyond that next bus stop.'

Manton drove past it and parked up a side turning. They got out and walked back.

Mendolia's flat was on the top floor of a block which had been completed shortly before the war. The mildly lecherous chairman of the company that had built it had designed the flat in question for his own convenient use and had provided it with a separate entrance and private lift. After all this trouble it was deplorable fortune that his wife had to find out about its existence and so vitiate its promising future.

The street door, which opened into a tiny lobby, was locked, but Manton was soon able to open it with one of the keys he'd brought with him. The lift was already down and awaited them with doors apart. They stepped inside and pressed a button labelled 'UP'. The doors closed with soft purpose, and a mild hum was the only sign that they were then upward borne.

When the doors opened they stepped out into another lobby, though one rather larger than that downstairs. It was richly carpeted and had upholstered wall benches on the sides. Ahead was a vermilion door with a bell push on the right.

Manton walked across and pressed it vigorously. From within a disembodied buzzing could be heard. Otherwise no sound at all came to their ears, and after a while Manton once more selected a key from his bunch.

Inside, the flat was in complete darkness, with no light com-

129

ing from beneath any of the doors that led off the hall in which
they now found themselves. Manton played the beam of his
torch from door to door and then moved stealthily over to one
on their right and opened it. It was the bathroom, resplendent
with thick pink carpet and gleaming fittings in black and white
and chromium. The shelf by the hand-basin which would
normally have harboured toothbrushes and the like, was bare.
Swift drew Manton's attention to it.

'M'mmm, looks as though he's done a bunk,' Manton said.
'We'll take a quick glance around.'

The next door that they tried opened into the living-room. A
faint smell of cigarette smoke hung in the air. The curtains were
drawn back and Manton walked quickly over to the window
and pulled them across.

'O.K., let's have the light on.'

The room was lushly furnished and in keeping with the bathroom. It made Swift feel that he had strayed on to an exotic
film set. Drawn up before a false fireplace was a huge sofa of
cavernous depths, at one end of which the cushions were
slightly flattened. Swift found himself staring at them and
wondering how many times Pamela and Mendolia had sat there
together.

'Come on, we'll try the remainder of the rooms,' Manton said,
leading the way out into the hall again.

Dining-room, kitchen and small dressing-room were examined in quick succession, but told them nothing, other than that
no one was at home. Manton turned the handle of the last door
and walked into what had to be the bedroom. The thin beam of
his torch prodded the darkness and roamed over the room, coming to rest finally on the bed. It was a large double one and over
on its far side was the unmistakable outline of a body.

Almost before Swift had taken in the scene, the room was
plunged into darkness.

'Stay here, I'm going round the other side,' Manton hissed in
his ear.

Swift's heart started to thump as he moved closer to the bed
and stood waiting for anything that might happen. A few
seconds later, a faint sound told him that Manton had now
reached the far side. Suddenly an eerie half light broke the darkness—Manton had switched on his torch and was cupping the
beam with his hand.

Straining furiously, Swift stared till he felt his eyes would drop out of his head. Then, it was all he could do not to hurl himself forward on to the bed.

Lying there, with a masklike expression and still as in death, was Pamela.

It seemed that hours passed before he saw Manton put out a hand and pick up something from the bedside table. A moment later he had returned to Swift's side. Holding out a small round carton, he said:

'Sleeping tablets. Looks like an overdose, whoever she is.' Only as Manton now spoke did Swift detect the quiet rhythm of Pamela's breathing. 'We'd better try to rouse her.'

Standing rooted to the same spot, with globules of cold sweat starting to trickle down his flanks, Swift watched Manton turn on the light and go back round to Pamela's side of the bed. Bending over her, he shook her gently by the shoulder. Nothing happened, and after a pause he did so again, this time more vigorously. Without opening her eyes, she put up a hand and let it fall loosely on the covers. It was several seconds before she stirred again. Then she opened her eyes to stare vacantly up into Manton's face. A moment later she let out a piercing scream.

'Who are you?' She sat up in bed and looked frantically about her, then catching sight of Swift, who was standing in a state of petrified immobility: 'What are you doing here?'

Fortunately Manton appeared to notice nothing untoward. He said:

'We're the police. We're looking for Mendolia. Where is he?'

'He's not here.'

'Where's he gone?'

'I don't know.'

'Well, who are *you*?'

She threw Swift a covert glance before replying.

'I'm a friend of his.'

'Name?'

'Pamela . . . Pamela Stoughton.'

'What are you doing in his flat?'

'I've told you, I'm a friend of his.'

'Do you feel all right?'

'How do you mean?'

'How many of these things have you taken?' Manton held out the carton of sleeping tablets.

'I took two. I'm not really used to them. They're . . . they're

Joe's. He left them for me, as I've not been sleeping very well
lately.'

'When did you last see Mendolia?'

'Yesterday.' She lay back and yawned. 'At least, what's the
time?'

'Nearly one o'clock.'

'It was the day before yesterday, then.'

'And you've no idea where he's gone?' She shook her head.
'When are you expecting him back?'

'In three or four days.'

'Are you stopping here till he returns?'

She threw Swift another quick glance.

'Oh, no!'

'Where do you live?'

'Down Wimbledon way.'

'O.K., we'll leave you to your sleep.' He put the sleeping
tablets back on the bedside table. 'I'd be careful with these
things. They can be dangerous unless you take them under doc-
tors orders.' Manton walked round the foot of the bed to the
door. 'Come on, we'll be on our way,' he said to Swift, who was
standing feeling as though all his insides had been scooped out.
'Good night.' He switched off the bedroom light and closed the
door behind them.

'Could have been a rather tricky situation,' he said dryly as
they descended in the lift. 'Fortunately she was still a bit dopy,
or we might have found ourselves on the spot—wandering about
her boy-friend's flat in the middle of the night without a warrant or anything.'

When they got downstairs again, Manton decided to knock
up the caretaker, who, scared and truculent by turn, grudgingly
conceded that he'd seen Mendolia about eleven o'clock the previous morning, but not since. He had then been flinging a
couple of suitcases into his car.

Leaving the block of flats, Manton and Swift set forth on a
quick round of Mendolias Soho establishments. It was getting
on for half past one before they arrived at the first, where the
atmosphere had long since formed itself into thick layers of
smoke and body odour. But neither here nor at the succeeding
ones they visited did it appear that Mendolia had been seen
within the past forty-eight hours. The men to whom they
talked spoke, for the most part, in nods, shrugs and laconic
phrases addressed invariably at the ceiling, their fingertips or

any other inanimate object on which the gaze could be focused.

At one of them, however, a waiter significantly let on that he'd heard a rumour that day to the effect that the boss had sold his interest in the place. He added that as long as someone continued to pay him his money, he didn't care who owned the dump.

It was after three o'clock before Swift climbed into bed. He ached all over with physical exhaustion and his mind was blurred to every thought save one. Roy Cordari's murderer had somehow got to be hunted down.

CHAPTER NINETEEN

Among the assets of youth are resilience and a capacity for quick recovery. It was these which enabled Swift to wake up at seven o'clock feeling refreshed and ready to face a new day.

By half past he had breakfasted and was on his way back to Mendolia's flat. Before all else he'd got to have things out with Pamela.

'As if I couldn't have guessed,' she said on opening the front door and beholding him. He gave her a wry smile and followed her into the living-room, where she poured him out a cup of coffee. 'Want anything to eat?'

'No, thanks. This'll be fine.' He held the cup in his hand, obviously ill at ease. 'Now about Mendolia.' Pamela sighed. She'd been expecting cross-examination of a more personal nature.

'He's gone away for a few days.'

'So you said last night. Where to?'

'I don't know.'

'Sounds very much as if he's skipped out of the country.'

'Not in the sense you mean.'

'How do you know?'

'I just do.'

Swift stared at her pensively awhile. Then he said:

'I thought you and I were batting for the same side: namely to run Roy's murderer to ground.'

'As far as I'm concerned, we still are,' she replied a trifle stiffly.

'Well, why are you holding out on me over Mendolia?'

'I'm doing no such thing. I've told you what I know: namely that he's gone away for a few days. I couldn't find out where to.'

'How do you know he's coming back, then: that he's not left these shores for good?'

She bit her lip and seemed torn by indecision. Eventually she faced him with a level gaze and said:

'I'm sorry, Kevin. I can't tell you everything just yet. But I promise that I will soon.'

'Perhaps you can at least tell me what you were doing here last night?' he asked in a suddenly abrasive tone.

'You wanted me to find out all I could about his activities, didn't you? Well, what better opportunity than to have a snoop around when he's away?'

'For which purpose, I gather, he thoughtfully provided you with a key and a pass to his bed?' Swift observed in a withering tone. 'There wasn't likely to be much to find here in those circumstances, was there?' He stared at her balefully.

Pamela bit nervously at the cuticle of her thumb. She could see that almost anything she said would expose her to further thrusting questions, and this she wanted to avoid. Speaking quietly and with a certain air of contrition, she said:

'I'm sorry, Kevin. But please believe that nothing I could tell you at the moment would assist the police in any way.'

'Maybe you're right.' He appeared mollified by her tone and his forehead crinkled anxiously. 'But are you the best judge of that?'

'Yes,' she replied before he had time to go on.

'Did Mendolia tell you nothing before he left?'

'As a matter of fact he did. He said that you should concentrate on West End Court and that the key to the whole case lay there.'

'That all?'

'Yes.'

'Just the sort of thing he might say to try to throw us off his scent while he's making a getaway.'

Pamela appeared to think hard over this. In the end she shrugged her shoulders and said stonily:

'That's what he said. And if you're really interested in finding out who killed Roy, I'd have thought you'd be pleased to have such a lead.'

'If I believed it, I probably would be.'

With a sudden impulsive gesture, she put a hand out and took one of his.

'Kevin, it is true. I happen to *know* it is. The only thing is I can't tell you, for the present, why I know. Please believe me and please follow it up. I *know*, yes, *know*, you'll be on the right lines if you do. Mendolia heard it from a reliable source. It isn't just a trick to get himself out of trouble, as you seem to think. It's a genuine tip-off.' She looked at him imploringly. 'And in a day or so I'll be able to tell you why I'm so certain of it.'

As he journed back to the Yard, Swift felt himself truly caught between the devil and the deep. For now that Cordari was dead, responsibility for protecting Pamela from all the dangers of the assignment they'd thrust at her was his alone. But her present attitude was, to say the least, disquieting. Moreover, any official action was out of the question. The thought of trying to explain matters to Manton at this stage was too forbidding to be seriously contemplated. Particularly after last night.

He tried to assuage his anxiety by recalling that she'd not, after all, asked for assistance nor expressed any fears for her safety. On the contrary, she'd appeared wholly confident of coping with events in her own way.

For the first time, however, he wondered whether the original idea of enlisting her aid had been quite such a good one as it had seemed; furthermore, what action he would take if she did become involved in a sudden crisis and cried out for help.

It was in an uneasy mood that he regained the Yard and waited for Manton to come in.

He was sent for about twenty minutes later. When he entered the room, Manton was yawning cavernously.

'How are you feeling?' he asked, when he was able to speak.

'All right, sir,' Swift replied in a tone which gave nothing away.

'They've cabled the contents of the letter found on Heath's body. I asked them to do so pending the arrival of the document itself.'

'What's it say, sir?'

'We'll see in a moment. It's on its way up, now.'

Soon afterwards a young police cadet came in and handed Manton a piece of paper.

'You'd better come round and read it too,' Manton said, inviting Swift to his side. The document which he held in his hand was an international cable form. It read:

TEXT OF LETTER FOUND ON DEAD ENGLISHMAN GORDON HEATH. DEAR HEATH, YOUR LETTER WHICH ARRIVED THIS MORNING CAUSED ME CONSIDERABLE SURPRISE, NOT LEAST ON ACCOUNT OF ITS INSINUATIONS. HOWEVER, THE POINT IS THAT I AM NOT PREPARED TO EXTEND YOU FURTHER ASSISTANCE IN THE CIRCUMSTANCES AND YOU MUST DO AS YOU SEE FIT TO ACHIEVE YOUR OWN SALVATION. IN THE BELIEF THAT THE LEAST SAID THE BETTER, I AM YOURS SINCERELY, DROXFORD.

When both had had time to read it through, Manton looked up and said:

'Well?'

'There's only one thing to do, sir. Get along to West End and find out from Lord Droxford the circumstances in which he came to write it.'

'I agree.' Manton consulted his watch. It said twenty minutes to ten. 'If we go now, we'll be able to talk to him before the court sits.'

Suiting action to words, he sprang up, tucked the cable away in an inside pocket, and followed by Swift, shot out of the room and down the corridor.

It soon appeared that this was likely to prove the speediest section of their journey, as Manton looked out impatiently at a cohort of red buses that hemmed them in half-way up Regent Street.

'If we don't move next time the lights turn green, we'll get out and walk,' he said with exasperation.

By the time they'd arrived at court, he'd had occasion to repeat this about once every fifty yards.

Following Manton into the building, Swift paused to give Susannah a look. She was playing a number from 'Porgy and Bess' and staring straight ahead of her in the way that she always did.

Lord Droxford hadn't yet arrived and Manton asked to see Mr. Astbury, who had so far broken with routine as to arrive a quarter of an hour early.

'I'd very much like to have a word with Lord Droxford before he goes into court, sir.'

'I expect he'll see you. What's it about, or shouldn't I ask that?'

'It's to do with our inquiries into your missing defendants,' Manton said neutrally.

'Well, don't keep him long. It's difficult enough to get through the work when we start on time. And the loss of five or ten minutes can be disastrous.'

'It shouldn't take long.'

While they spoke, Mr. Astbury was doing half a dozen other things as well, apparently able to divide his attention quite efficiently into several equal parts. Busily initialling a sheaf of documents before him, he said without looking up:

'How's it going ? Got anyone lined up yet?'

Manton shook his head. 'I'm afraid it's going to be a slow job.'

'And possibly fruitless as well?'

Manton thought he detected a faint note of mockery in the question. 'Oh, no, we'll solve it all right in time,' he said, nevertheless wishing he were as confident as his words sounded.

Mr. Astbury looked up, and his eyes, glinting sardonically behind his spectacles, met Manton's.

'That's good news, anyway.' He suddenly cocked an ear. 'I think I heard Lord Droxford go into his room then. Hang on a moment and I'll find out if he'll see you.'

He left the room. Manton and Swift stood waiting, each silently occupied with his own thoughts.

'Tell them that the clue to the case lies at West End Court.' That was what Mendolia had told Pamela to pass on to the police and what now went through Swift's mind as he gazed out of the window. His eye fell casually on the legend

REX TURNBULL & CO.
SOLICITORS

written in black letters edged in gold on one of the windows opposite. The lower pane of the window on which this legend appeared was frosted and so thwarted prying eyes. Two windows along was Rex Turnbull's own office. Here a long white gauze curtain achieved a similar object.

As Swift stared across, a thought began to form in his mind. Mendolia's hint could easily have been meant to include the advocates who practised at the court—in particular his own solicitor, Rex Turnbull, who not only had the major practice there but had been concerned in all but one of the cases involving the missing defendants. He looked at Manton and wondered whether he shouldn't tell him what he'd learnt from Pamela, even though it would mean explaining her part and risking an almighty choking off. Reprimand now or the boot later, that was what it probably amounted to.

Even as he weighed the matter, Mr. Astbury returned to the room and the decision was made for him. The moment for explanation had slipped away.

'Lord Droxford'll see you now.' He led the way out again and ushered the two officers into the room next door.

'This is Detective Constable Swift, sir,' Manton said, as they entered. The magistrate was standing in front of the fireplace, looking grave to the point of forbidding. He flashed Swift the merest glance at the introduction. Swift closed the door and took up a position with his back to it.

'Yes, Superintendent, what is it you want? I have to be in court in ten minutes.'

Manton decided to play it the same way. Brisk and formal. He pulled the cable out of his pocket and laid it open on the corner of the desk where Lord Droxford could easily see it.

'I think this is the text of a letter you wrote, sir—a letter that was found on Heath's dead body yesterday.'

'Heath! Dead?'

'Yes, sir; he died yesterday.'

'Good gracious! Under what circumstances?'

'He shot himself,' said Manton, watching him keenly.

Lord Droxford contrived to look like a colonel who has just heard that the platoon of troops he ordered into battle has been wiped out. Responsible for their dispatch, yes: for their destruction, certainly not.

'Well, what is it you want to know?' he asked, straightening his shoulders and meeting Manton's gaze.

'It looks as though this letter of yours, sir, may have had something to do with his taking his life. In the first place, it's obviously in answer to one you received from him. Would you care to say what was in that?'

'This is a most disagreeable situation. But my conscience is clear and I have absolutely no intention of letting it be thought that I was in any degree responsible for this unfortunate man's death; since I was most certainly not.' Following this categorical pronouncement, he went on: 'In those circumstances I'm prepared to lay bare at least part of my soul for your inspection.' He motioned a finger towards the cable. 'I wrote that letter last

Monday, the same day on which I received one from Heath. He said in his that the police had been to see him about the matter which led to his resignation as usher of this court and also in connection with some more recent indiscretion. And he asked me if I would stick by him in the event of his finding himself in serious trouble and also if I could let him have some money. Some more money, might have been a more accurate way of putting it.'

'Have you often lent him money, sir?'

'I don't lend money to anyone. I don't believe in it. I have on occasions given away certain sums, however, including some to Heath.'

'How recently have you sent him any, sir?' Manton asked in a calculated casual tone.

'I think I sent him a little at Christmas. That must have been the last time.'

'How used you to remit it? In Treasury notes?'

'Good heavens, no! What an impracticable suggestion! If you must know, I did it through my wife's French account and got my brother-in-law out in Algeria to give it to him.'

There was a pause. Then Manton picked up the cable and appeared to re-read it.

'What precisely were you referring to, sir, when you wrote of "insinuations"?'

'Perhaps I was a bit hasty over that. Looking back on it now, I think I may have misunderstood the tenor of his letter. But at the time, it struck me that he was suggesting I was under some form of obligation to help him out. And quite frankly I took strong exception to it. Hence my somewhat uncompromising reply.'

'Can you recall the exact words he used, sir?' Manton asked patiently.

Lord Droxford furrowed his brow and stared hard at the floor between his feet as he gently rocked himself to and fro on his heels. Then throwing back his head he said:

'No, I can't. All I remember is the impression they made on me at the time, which, as I say, was that he seemed to think he was asking no more than his due.'

'I see, sir,' Manton said, nodding in an understanding way. 'Are you surprised to hear he's committed suicide?'

'Surprised? Well, no—on consideration, I can't say I am.'

'It's clear from our inquiries, sir, that he was the agent of some criminal outfit in this country, which has been connected with the disappearance of defendants from this court.'

'Of that, I know nothing, of course. He wasn't specific in his letter about the nature of his present trouble, and I had no intention of becoming involved in it. In fact, I considered I'd given him all the help he should need and I was even beginning to wonder whether I hadn't done too much for him.'

It was at this moment that there was a knock on the door, which then immediately opened to reveal Plowman. He was wearing his black usher's gown and took a step into the room.

'The court is ready, sir,' he said in a properly deferential tone. Though he obviously couldn't help noticing Manton and Swift, he showed no sign of embarrassment at their presence, which might have been expected to afford an uncomfortable reminder of his interview the previous evening. At all events he gave them no heed and appeared wholly unconcerned at seeing them there.

'I'm coming now,' Lord Droxford said. 'Just wait outside a moment, would you?' Plowman withdrew. 'Is that all, Superintendent?' As he spoke, he started to move towards the door.

'You've no reason to suspect any of your court staff of being mixed up with anything criminal, have you, sir?' Manton asked, in a tone that was faintly apologetic.

'Good gracious, no! We like to think we're a particularly efficient and happily run court—and not without some justification. From myself down, we all pull our weight. Ask Mr. Astbury. Ask any of the jailer's staff; indeed, ask any of the advocates who come and practise here, and I'm sure they'll all tell you the same thing.' He buttoned up his dark, double-breasted jacket and smoothed the front with his hands. 'I really must go now.'

Manton and Swift were about to follow him out of the room when Manton suddenly remembered the cable and went back for it.

'I think we might spend a few minutes in court before we go,' he said as they made their way downstairs.

By the time they entered the court, Lord Droxford had already started on his morning list of cases.

Manton and Swift tiptoed in and stood against one of the side walls. There was the usual procession of tarts and drunks whom P.C. Tredgold marshalled in and out with practised skill. The first case of substance concerned a well-dressed man of middle age, who, it transpired, was charged with importuning.

Having steered him safely into the dock, Tredgold announced him in ringing tones. After Mr. Astbury had read out the charge, the man cast the jailer a beseeching look.

'This defendant is asking for an adjournment, sir, as his solicitor can't be here this morning. He wants to have Mr. Turnbull appear for him, but he's not available today.'

'Does that mean that all Mr. Turnbull's cases are going to be subject to postponement?' Lord Droxford asked.

'He's only in one other as far as I know, sir,' Tredgold replied.

Without further comment, Lord Droxford complied with the request and the defendant slipped thankfully away. Manton nudged Swift and the two of them went out into the jailer's office.

'What's this about Mr. Turnbull not being around today?' Manton asked.

'Search me, sir,' Tredgold said, in a preoccupied tone. 'All I know is what that last bloke told me. 'Scuse me now, sir.' He moved away and beckoned to a dignified old lady. 'Here you, Clara. It's your turn now.' Pushing her before him, he disappeared with her through the swing door which led into court. The last that Swift heard was, 'Charge number seven, sir, Clara Best,' as the jailer's voice came floating back to them. The odds were, Swift reflected, she was charged with some most improbable offence. Elderly ladies invariably were—especially the dignified-looking ones.

'We'll go over the road and find out what's happened to Rex Turnbull,' Manton said, leading the way out of the building.

Susannah greeted them with 'Only a Rose' as they emerged. Swift peeped in her tin as they went by. There was nothing in it, but then he remembered her habit of emptying it as soon as anyone dropped her a coin.

They climbed the stairs which led to the solicitor's office. The girl at the inquiry office said that Mr. Turnbull wasn't in at the moment, but beyond that was non-committal. Manton asked to see his chief clerk, and after some delay a rather harassed-looking man came out of one of the rooms along the passage and approached them.

'I'm sorry, Superintendent, but Mr. Turnbull isn't available at the moment.'

'So I gathered over at court. He seems to have gone away very suddenly,' Manton observed.

'Yes, yes, but I hope he'll be back tomorrow. He had to leave in a hurry and everything's just a bit chaotic. I haven't yet had a chance to get across to court and explain to Mr. Astbury.'

'You needn't worry. He already knows. One of your potential clients asked for an adjournment on that account.'

'Oh, yes, that man charged with importuning. He came in here before the court sat and I explained to him that Mr. Turnbull was away.'

'I can see it must make life difficult when you arrive one morning to find that your principal has been unexpectedly called away on urgent business?'

'Indeed, yes. No warning at all. But I'm sure he'll be back tomorrow and you'll be able to see him then if you call in again. Unless there's anything I can do for you meanwhile.'

'Would you be knowing where Mr. Turnbull has gone?' Manton asked in as guileless a tone as he could.

'I'm afraid I can't discuss my principal's private affairs with you,' the clerk said, trying to soften the refusal with a quick nervous smile.

'No, I suppose not,' Manton said thoughtfully. 'But would I be far out in thinking that his absence is to do with a client named . . . Mendolia?'

'Really!' the clerk expostulated in obvious embarrassment. 'It's most improper of you to ask me to divulge such matters. I can't possibly answer a question like that.'

'All right, don't worry,' Manton said soothingly, smothering the temptation to add: 'You have.'

Leaving the solicitor's office, the two Yard men turned and walked in the direction of Sirena Street.

'Mendolia and Rex Turnbull both mysteriously vanished,' Manton remarked at large, as they strode along. 'I think we'd better have a careful, but unofficial, watch kept out for them. But I wish to God I knew why they've suddenly decided to disappear.'

Once again Swift mentally tossed up whether to tell Manton about Pamela, and once again the opportunity went by unseized. If only he could quietly work out some of the implications of recent events, it would help him to make up his mind. If only he could be sure about Pamela herself. But somehow he could never get beyond seeing the individual trees—moreover, many of these looked different each time he studied them—and the wood itself remained obstinately shapeless.

It was some time in the middle of the afternoon that he was suddenly struck by one of those blinding thoughts, which are frequently regurgitated from the subconscience for no apparent reason. Only, this one really was staggering. It caused him to halt literally in his tracks and for a moment or two concentrate with such intensity that the world around him receded.

When he became aware of himself once more, he was trembling with excitement. It was something unwittingly said that now stood out in his mind as a possible clue to the whole affair. Where Cordari and the others had met their deaths was certain. Why they'd been killed had been reasonably inferential for some time. But who had murdered them had until this moment been an unfathomed mystery.

Making his way down to the canteen, he chose a table to himself over in a far corner. A sudden vision of what had happened was one thing, what to do about it quite another. Further investigation was obviously required before an arrest was possible and it was a matter of deciding whether to apprise Manton now or first to burrow a bit deeper himself.

By the time he had drunk a cup of tea, his mind was made up. After all, had he not sworn to avenge Cordari's death—Roy Cordari with whom he'd been so closely linked by the comradely bonds of their assignment? That now seemed a very long while back, but its effect on Swift's outlook had been profound. For weeks, his horizon had been bounded entirely by the scope of the present inquiry. He didn't try to see beyond it or wonder what might come next. He didn't even bother to care. He realized that if he made a mess of things by acting on his own, he might well be chucked out of the Force, but that was a risk he was prepared to take. The dominant factor in reaching his decision had been that he owed it to Roy Cordari's memory to display some personal initiative in tracking down his killer.

He spent the rest of that evening preparing his plan and making the inquiries necessary to its fulfilment.

He managed to get off duty about half past seven and set out immediately for his destination. He found the street he was looking for quite easily and walked quickly down one side and up the other, taking special note of the one but last house on the left-hand side. It was a small detached villa standing in about an eighth of an acre of garden and surrounded by a high overgrown privet hedge. There was no sign of life. The odds were, Swift knew from his inquiries, that there was no one at home;

but he was taking no chances. At the opposite end of the street, he'd noticed a small café, and he now retired there and managed to get himself a seat in the window from which he was able to keep a good watch on all movement.

In half an hour's time, it would be getting dark and if by then he'd not seen anyone enter the house and there were no lights on inside, it should be safe to go in.

As he sat smoking his pipe, drinking a cup of ill-made coffee and pretending to scan an evening paper, he was oppressed by the unreality of the situation. Here he was, an officer of the Metropolitan Police, on his own personal responsibility, about to break into a private citizen's home. There could hardly be a shorter cut to expulsion, if not something more serious. But his only reaction was to smile wryly to himself. 'What will be will be' were the words of a popular song which seemed aptly to fit the situation.

He looked in the other direction and saw that the buses passing the end now had their interior lights on. It was time to make a move.

He approached the house along the opposite pavement and slowed his pace when he was near enough to observe it covertly. No lights had been turned on and there was still no sign of life within.

In case anyone should be watching him, he walked nonchalantly across the street, and on reaching the gate took a quick look round before slipping inside in one noiseless movement. Standing in the cover of the hedge, he scanned the house once more. He decided to take the path which led towards the garden at the back. It was just possible that someone was there, pottering about. He moved stealthily to a point where the path ran out from beside the house and he could survey the whole garden. It was quite empty.

Reassured that he had the premises to himself, he set about a closer study of the windows. One of the fanlights of the kitchen window was open and he nodded to himself with satisfaction. This was better than he'd expected.

By standing on the outside sill and putting his hand through the fanlight he'd be able to open one of the casement windows below and climb through.

A trifle self-consciously he pulled a pair of cotton gloves from his pockets and put them on. A minute later he was inside the house. It was thoughtful of someone to have left that window open, as he'd be able to leave the same way and nobody need ever be any the wiser.

There was just sufficient light inside to enable him to see his way around without bumping into awkward bits of furniture.

He found his way into the hall and then upstairs. There it was the front bedroom that claimed his attention—indeed, investigation showed it to be the only bedroom on that floor.

A ten-minute search, however, revealed nothing of significance and he began to feel the onset of bitter frustration.

But there was still the back room to be gone over. A small bureau in it looked promising. Two of its lower drawers overflowed with a miscellany of odds and ends when he pulled them open, but the bottom one was locked. Turning next to the pigeon-holes, he quickly ran through their contents. He was on the point of turning his attention elsewhere when he stared again at the piece of paper in his hand. It was a receipt dated a few days before the shelter discovery—and it related to the purchase of a pair of rubber boots.

His heart thumped with excitement as he tucked it carefully away in his pocket. Now he was really certain that he was on the right track.

A further quick survey satisfied him that there was no sign of any rubber boots in the house and that the bottom bureau drawer was the only piece of furniture which still defied search.

Switching off the small pencil-beam torch which he'd been compelled to use during the last quarter of an hour, he bent down to study the possibilities of forcing the drawer open. He'd taken so many risks by now that one more seemed of little consequence.

But first he'd try a few of the keys he'd brought along with him.

Thus engrossed, he heard nothing save his own heartbeats and steady breathing: not even the quick swish of heavy rubber before it caught him at the base of the head and plunged him into a world of surrealistically exploding lights.

When he came to, it was quite dark. His head ached abominably and he was completely trussed up. His legs were knotted together just below the knees and again round the ankles, and his wrists efficiently bound behind his back. A piece of adhesive tape had been stuck over his mouth.

The house was as still as the night itself.

145

Now he really was in a mess, he reflected angrily. Anger, indeed, was his dominant emotion. With an almighty heave he managed to roll himself over. As he did so, his head caught something sharp and he ground his teeth at the stab of pain. As his eyes began to get accustomed to the darkness, he saw that it was an open drawer against which he had bumped—the open bottom bureau drawer.

Swift had always been sceptical of the ease with which heroes of adventure stories in similar plights to his appeared to free themselves. But now as anger and determination took possession of his body, he rolled and wriggled in paroxysms of frenzy. Unmindful of pain and striving to the point of utter exhaustion, he found his bonds could slowly be worked loose.

It must have taken him a full two hours before he was eventually free. The first thing he did was to look at his watch. It showed a quarter to three. Five hours had passed since he'd been knocked out.

A quick search revealed that there was no one in the house.

There was a police station not more than half a mile away; he must get there as soon as possible. Leaving the house he directed his groggy steps along the silent street. Quite suddenly he halted and felt anxiously in his jacket pocket, then with a heavy sigh of relief he set off again. At least, he still had the receipt for the rubber boots.

The main road on which he turned left was equally deserted and stretched ahead of him with heart-breaking straightness. He hurried as best he could, but several times had to stop and put out a quick hand to steady himself when the scenery began to behave as though an earthquake was in progress. Long before he got there, he could see the lantern which hung above the police station entrance, shining its unmistakable and rather ghostlike blue.

The sergeant on duty listened impassively to Swift's story. He was used to hearing stranger ones than this and had long ago learnt that it was always best to reserve judgment. When at the end it occurred to Swift to produce his warrant card, he sprang into immediate action.

'I must get through to Superintendent Manton immediately,' Swift went on feverishly. 'He lives somewhere near Purley.'

'Right, you sit down a moment and I'll look up his number for you.' A moment later, he said: 'Come and sit at the desk over here. I'll dial it for you.' He handed over the receiver.

As Swift sat with it pressed furiously to his ear, listening to the distant, impersonal brr-brr, he tried in his mind's eye to picture Manton waking up and getting out of bed to answer it. Every time, however, he got him downstairs and to the point of stretching out a hand to the 'phone, which he mentally saw situated in the hall, nothing at all would happen save a maddening continuance of the sound, and he'd feel compelled to start all over again. So concentrated was his mind on this game that when suddenly the ringing did cease and he heard Manton's voice he was wholly unprepared for it, having, at that moment, got him still in the bedroom and groping for his slippers.

'It's Swift, sir. I'm speaking from Hounslow police station,' he said, trying to suppress a sudden, overwhelming sense of despair. Though he'd rehearsed just what he would say, it now came out all different as he stammered and fought to explain himself in half-completed sentences. When he stopped, there was a long silence before Manton, who had listened throughout without comment, spoke. At length he said:

'But you didn't see who knocked you out?'

'No, sir.'

'Not even a glimpse?'

'I'm afraid not, sir.'

There was another long pause, while Manton thought and Swift at his end sat waiting. Indeed, it seemed to Swift that he had time not only to reflect fully on the past, but also to take in a rueful survey of the future, before Manton spoke again. When he did so, it was in the tone of one who would clearly have liked to have had more faith in the decision he'd reached.

'O.K., we'd better do something about it immediately. I'll get through to the Yard and give instructions, and meet you there in an hour's time.'

Soon the teleprinters went into stuttering action. Police all over the country were alerted to watch out for a man aged approximately forty-eight, six feet tall, weighing fifteen stone, with brown hair brushed straight back, grey eyes and a fresh complexion—and answering to the name of Arnold Plowman.

London was just starting to come to life when Swift reached the Yard. The streets were being washed down and the indomitable army of office cleaners was on the march.

Manton arrived a few minutes after him.

'Pity you never got a glimpse of the chap who cracked you

147

over the head,' he said, almost as soon as they were together.

'It must have been Plowman, though, sir,' Swift said desperately.

'Looks like it. Anyway, we've got good enough reason to rope him in. About this drawer that was locked, but later open and empty, you believe it was full of cash, eh?'

Swift nodded. 'Yes, sir. All the money he's had from the victims he's murdered in the shelter.'

Manton appeared thoughtful. Then he said:

'Let's hear again what it was that put you on to him. You weren't very explicit on the 'phone and I didn't really follow all you were trying to say.'

Swift took a deep breath and gently felt at his lips, which were still uncomfortably sore from the piece of tape that had been stuck over his mouth.

'You remember, sir, Susannah telling us that the last few times he'd collected forty-two pounds from her and his saying that he used to take along an envelope to put the money into after deducting his commission?'

'Yes, very clearly.'

'Well, sir, it's all a matter of arithmetic. Fifteen per cent of forty-two is something between six and seven pounds. He said it was to the nearest pound above.'

'Yes, go on. I'm with you so far,' Manton said, when Swift paused.

'If you take seven pounds from forty-two, you have thirty-five, which according to him he remitted to the mysterious man in seven five-pound notes.' Comprehension was beginning to dawn in Manton's eyes. 'And one of those two notes must have been that badly damaged one.'

'Which he sent to Heath as payment for posting one of the letters back to England,' Manton broke in keenly. 'Yes, you're right. You must be right.'

Considerably encouraged by Manton's reaction Swift continued with the earnestness of the special pleader.

'If I am, sir, it's pretty obvious that Plowman is himself the owner of the Sirena Street property, and that he told us all that rigmarole the other evening to throw us off the trail and make us believe that he was a mere pawn in some racket run by a powerful off-stage villain.' He saw slight doubt clouding Manton's brow. 'After all, sir, it's quite a subtle idea when you're in a tight corner to give things a false slant, which is precisely what he did. Supposing he hadn't come to collect the money that evening and we'd eventually got on to him, as we should have done, he'd have found it far more difficult to explain himself then. But by coming forward as he did and feeding us that plausible spiel, he went a long way to disarming us of suspicion in advance.'

'Whether or not he owns the house in Sirena Street, he's still got to explain about the pound note,' Manton conceded, if declining for the moment to endorse all Swift's inferences. 'He could never have foreseen the incredible fluke that was to turn it into such a damning piece of evidence against him.' Manton's mind drifted away in contemplation of its astonishing odyssey. From Tredgold to Mendolia to Susannah to Plowman to Heath to Swift and back to Susannah it had wound its devious way. Recalling his thoughts, he stared hard at his young assistant for a moment or two. 'But let's not forget that Plowman isn't the only one to have suddenly disappeared without explanation. Indeed, until he fails to report for work this morning, I shan't be really satisfied that he has at all.'

But if Manton wasn't sure about it, Swift had no doubts on that score. It was with complete confidence that he accompanied Manton to West End Court a few hours later.

'Plowman about?' Manton asked P.C. Tredgold, as he thrust his way up to the jailer at one minute before half past ten.

'No, he's not arrived. Can't think what's happened to him. Usually gets a message through if he's sick.'

Swift tried to give Manton an I-told-you-so-sir look, but failed to obtain his attention. He followed him into court, where, with relief, they observed that at least Lord Droxford and Mr. Astbury hadn't joined the disappearing throng. Nor had Susannah, who was at her pitch outside playing as though life had never been less eventful.

But Manton was obviously still worried, and in the end managed to imbue Swift with doubt and a growing sense of frustration. When Manton suggested he should take two or three hours off and get some rest, he accepted with alacrity. Rest, however, was not the use to which he proposed putting the time.

Giving Pamela's phone number as the one where he could be reached if required, he hurried down to Wimbledon determined to force the truth out of her by means fair or ungentlemanly.

She was holding a glass of orange juice in her hand when she answered the door.

'Oh, hello, Kevin,' she said, adding agreeably: 'You look a trifle battered.'

'I've been a trifle battered,' he replied grimly, stepping inside and closing the door behind him.

She looked at him coolly for a moment before leading the way into the living-room.

'I imagine you've only come to talk about one thing.'

He nodded. 'You're darned right I have. You've got to tell me everything you know about Mendolia. I don't think you realize how serious it is to withhold information in a matter of this sort.'

'But I have told you already, Kevin. He had nothing to do with the murder of those men who disappeared from court.'

'That's not good enough, I've got to know more—*now*.'

He cursed as the 'phone started ringing and she went across the room to answer it.

'It's for you,' she said slowly, holding the receiver out to him with a surprised expression.

Taking it from her, he said in his most formal tone:

'Detective Constable Swift speaking.'

'Superintendent Manton here. I've just heard they've caught Plowman. At Bristol Airport as he was about to board a 'plane for Dublin. He had over a thousand pounds on him in ready cash. They're holding him at the moment on a customs charge, and you and I must get down there as soon as possible. There's a train from Paddington in about an hour's time. Meet you at the end of the platform. O.K.?'

'Yes, sir,' Swift replied feebly, as he heard the line go dead. He turned to find Pamela watching him. 'I've got to go, but don't think that lets you out, because first you're going to tell me——'

'I couldn't help hearing your conversation,' she said, taking no notice of what he was saying. 'It seemed to confirm what I've told you. Namely, that Mendolia wasn't in this.'

Swift looked desperately at his watch. He only just had sufficient time to get to the station if he left immediately.

'O.K., Pamela, but as soon as I get back I'll be round here and then nothing less than an H-bomb will get me out before you've told me the whole truth.'

'By the time you get back, you'll have the man you want under lock and key and I mayn't be here.'

He stopped short in his flight towards the door.

'Not here? Where are you going? I must be able to see you when I come back.' A shyly attractive grin crossed his features. 'And I've also got a lot of other very important things to talk to you about.'

She studied him with a wistful air.

'I'd better tell you this now, Kevin,' she said with sudden decision. 'Joe Mendolia and I are going to be married. We're in love, Kevin; really in love.' When he seemed on the point of interrupting her, she hurried on: 'No, let me explain first before you say anything. You see, that's why I had to be even more certain than you that he had nothing to do with Roy's death. I was sure he hadn't but I had to be positive before I could commit myself.' Swift seemed hypnotized by her words and stood with lips parted and eyes fixed in an incredulous stare. 'If you feel like sneering—and I wouldn't really blame you if you did—let me just tell you that Joe's agreed to give up everything here and we're going to live abroad. That's how much he loves me!' Her mouth twisted into a self-deprecating smile. 'He's signed the pledge and it's no more rackety living for him. He and Mr. Turnbull are over in Ireland now seeing about buying a property. I'm flying to join him this evening.' She walked across to Swift. 'I'm afraid this has been a bit of a shock to you, Kevin, but you'll get over it.' She kissed him lightly on the lips and stepped back. 'And now you must rush or you'll never be at the station on time.'

It was not until several hours later when the train was well on its way to Bristol that Swift broke silence to express his tumultuous thoughts. Then, looking out at a field of placid Jersey cows, he said:

'I'll be b——d.'

EPILOGUE

The preparation of the case against Arnold Plowman took almost as long again and involved, among much else, the taking of scores of further statements. For Swift it also brought another trip to Algeria, where Mr. Roland greeted him with delight and tried out several fresh ruses to get members of his family on to Swift's expense account.

Eventually, however, Plowman was committed for trial at the Old Bailey on six charges of murder. The case against him there was presented as one of a cold-blooded opportunist who had killed for financial gain, with as little concern for his victims as a racecourse pickpocket.

It was established beyond doubt that his intention had been, on accumulating sufficient capital, to cut loose from his shrewish wife and disappear out of her life. It turned out that the house in Hounslow where they lived was hers and that the Sirena Street property, though his, having come to him under the intestacy of a bachelor uncle who had died some years before, was heavily mortgaged to a cousin by the name of da Suva, who now lived in Australia.

During the course of the trial, which lasted ten days, a whole parade of witnesses was called. Each came to fill in some small but vital part of the story and pass again on his way.

Only Manton and Swift maintained a daily vigil till it was all over and nothing further remained to be done. For Roy Cordari's death had been avenged.

>>> If you've enjoyed this book and would like to discover more great vintage crime and thriller titles, as well as the most exciting crime and thriller authors writing today, visit: >>>

The Murder Room
Where Criminal Minds Meet

themurderroom.com